THE BULLSHIT ARTIST

The Bullshit Artist

a novel

by Geoffrey Visgilio

This book is for my father.

PROLOGUE

*D*ear Ronan,

You take the stage like some kind of predatory animal, with full and terrifying command, an experience both exhilarating and wholly vicious. You open yourself, sharp scalpel cuts, precise, calculated, baring yourself to strangers in ways you'd never dare with yourself. Or with me.

You bleed for them. Live for them. Without them, you are hollow. An empty vessel. Useless, helpless, pathetic and lost, longing to be filled. To know purpose. To have something to give away. For the selfish, reckless, rakish prick that you are, you give away more of yourself than any charity or soup kitchen I've ever known. Motherfucking Theresa. That's who you will always be. To me.

I love you between my legs. These legs that captivated you at the Emmys after-party and have kept you wrapped up tight ever since. I love your mouth between my legs. Such a clever tongue.

All your words, the monologues and stories, the tales and jokes from which you earn your living are lost in the eager heat of my cassolette. All your passion and vitality that you beam to the audience is focused instead like a sun ray through a magnifying glass, melting me, burning me to cinders and ash, leaving me slick and spent and shaking. I am your sole audience, the only one who renders you truly speechless. And you will eat of me until I'm satisfied.

In every other moment in time, I hate you. White hot. Snake venom. A dram of poison. I hate you enough to touch myself when you leave me. I hate you enough to miss you when you're balls deep in another groupie or working your way through all the other fuckstars I introduced you to in the Valley. I hate your easy smile and that fake laugh that somehow isn't fake or that goddamned earnestness that made this whole fucking town fall so hard for you. That aw-shucks-miss that crushes distrust and makes you everyone's golden idol. I HATE it. I hate you. God help me, I hate you so much that I've come to love you a little bit and that makes me shakier inside than having your hateful face between my legs.

A dancer's legs, you once said. I have a dancer's legs and a poet's heart. The bit about the poet is bullshit and we both know it, part of your shtick, you always writing your act. Indeed, I've come to believe a part of you is always acting. A consummate bullshit artist, aren't you? You are made meaningful by the meaningless. You are made someone because you have enough of nothing to go around for everyone. If only they knew that the real joke was how seriously you take yourself. If they knew your inner critic was louder and colder and harsher than anything the tabloids throw at you. Do they know the two of your performances you hated the most were when you bombed on Fallon and then when you actually killed it on Kimmel. They can't know, but that you hated both your failure and your success with equal measure tells me everything I ever need to know about you, my dear.

Go now. Bury your father and drink deeply of that grief. Destroy the ones who are left, it's been a long time coming and *you can no longer avoid it. Show them no mercy, give them no quarter. You've barked for long enough, now bite. Tear them open and suckle the marrow from their splintered little bird bones. Bury the titan and assume the throne. Ruler for all time, once and future, you are king now. Make them know it.*

Besides, I only really love you when you leave me. If this is because I am a lover of shadows or so bent by the weight of my own gnarled psychology that this is the only way I know to get close to you, I cannot say. But I'm loving you harder this time. My heart is beating differently. My fingers are more urgent in the dark. I've never asked you for anything. Not once. I think that's the only reason this grim cemetery dance of ours has continued on. I know better than to ask of you.

But this one time, I don't ask. I demand. I know that look, the one you gave me when the car came to pick you up for the airport. The look no one can decipher, what Trevor Noah calls the Mona Lisa Man Puzzle. I know you think it ends for you now, that this is a terminal trip. One last trip home to settle your debts.

But I won't allow that. Do you hear me? Despite your efforts, you always surrender. So hear my demand: Return to me. It is my sole decree. Return to me. Our tango continues. We are locked like eagles entwined, falling and diving, snarls and claws, screeching and raw as our mating dance plunges us like missiles towards the earth.

Return to me, Ronan. We are unfinished. And I'm not done hating you yet.

Lovingly,

Margot

CHAPTER ONE

Long before the funeral and the car chase and more police than he could count, Ronan Besso sat in First Class nursing a shrieking banshee of a headache. He was still getting used to becoming a sudden celebrity. Not an A-lister, mind you, nothing so glamorous, but big enough for the rising comedian to fret over a juicy scandal threatening to topple it all just as quickly as it arrived. It was ten in the morning, West Coast time. He was running on two hours of rough sleep, relying on dark shades for anonymity and to hide the grizzled waste of his face after a week long coke binge. There was a time, not so long ago, when he could bounce back from these jaunts with a greasy cheeseburger and an Alka-Seltzer, but those days had passed. Approaching fifty was like stepping on a land mine, particularly unkind to fools and drunks, two personas which Ronan contentedly straddled.

He'd put the East Coast behind him ten years ago like slamming a door. The reverberation of it vibrated through him, shaking out into the very tips of his fingertips. It wasn't First Class cabins then, not even close. It was a beat-to-shit Ford Focus on its last legs and the few meager mementos gathered from a prior life. It was Motel 6 and more often than not, restless nights in a hot car with a pile of cigarette butts and puddles of cold coffee outside the driver's side door in the morning. It had been a messy extraction, like trying to scrape gum off the bottom of your shoe, and the landing hadn't been much better. But Ronan got out. Emancipated. Fit for a fresh start among palm trees and the Santa Ana winds.

He made good on his promise to never return. He missed his sister's wedding. He missed the birth of his nephew (The Immaculate Conception bears fruit!). He missed his oldest friend's funeral - a forgone conclusion after three tours in Afghanistan, an indifferent VA, and a steady descent into pills and then powder and then needles. He missed his high school and college reunions, both honoring him for his achievements as a rising star in the Hollywood sky. He'd almost been thrown out of both institutions and there were no tears shed among the faculty when he finally eked his way over the finish line to graduate. But, as never failed to both tickle and annoy him, Ronan was perpetually amazed how a Netflix special smoothed over a lot of rough edges, possessing the singular power of even altering memory in his favor.

As far as Ronan was concerned, the East Coast could rot in hell and the people there could go ahead and rot right on with it. He'd made good on his word and the west had been kinder to him than he ever imagined, surely more than he by any rights deserved. But here he was, pensive, strung out, and trying to sink deeper into the buttery leather of American Airlines Flight 784, seat 4A.

"Another, sir?"

The flight attendant's face was unmoved, anticipatory, purely professional. No judgment of his lifestyle in First Class. He smiled and nodded and the ritual unfolded for him.

He'd flown coach and standby enough to appreciate the clink of ice on real glass and pours from an actual bottle instead of cheap plastic nips. The rich had problems of their own and the lifestyle, Ronan fast discovered, was not without its trappings. But it was accepted you could drink like an adult at ten in the morning and that was something.

"Thank you," he said and took a deep swallow from the glass.

The tension in his jaw and neck relaxed some as the liquor worked its magic and he allowed himself to look around. The man next to him was fast asleep, snoring softly. He had on faded jeans and a red Hawaiian shirt with a gold Rolex submariner clamped around a hairy wrist - the official gold coast uniform of the recently divorced, probably a producer, agent, contract attorney, or what have you. He was even balding, tufts of hair sprouting from his ears, and his aftershave, despite the pronouncements of the official uniform, smelled drugstore cheap.

Across the aisle, Ronan felt someone looking at him. He turned to find a woman in her forties, pretty enough to not need all the construction work, but trapped in the lifestyle. Just like he was, wasn't she? Fake tits. He could spot them anywhere. After six months in LA, he was a crackerjack tit spotter, differentiating between real and plastic with uncanny accuracy. He admitted they looked great under clothes, but they always proved disappointing when finally unsheathed. He looked for the tell-tale marks of the face lift, but couldn't find them - her surgeon must be expensive. But there were traces of Botox and when she smiled at him, spotless veneers beamed at maximum wattage.

"I'm sorry for staring," she said. "Are you Ronan Besso?"

Recognition. Christ if that didn't take some getting used to. He didn't know how the A-listers could handle it. The first time it happened, he'd been flattered, tickled, almost unable to believe it really happened. It was the first time he knew he'd arrived. But he'd soured on it pretty quickly. *Say something funny!* That was the go-to. The on-the-spot, dance for us, do that thing you do demand from the rubes. After a while? The shit got old is what. The shit got old in a hurry. This woman, in her short skirt and expensive heels, seemed a little more sophisticated than the rabble, but he braced himself, grateful for dark glasses and the fortification of liquor over ice.

"Guilty, I'm afraid."

She reached across the aisle to swat at his arm. That was another part of it. The touching. Ronan couldn't count how many strangers would just grab him once he acknowledged them, like he was a puppy at a kindergarten. His arms, his face. The hugs, the kisses. Once a lady old enough to be his nana grabbed his crotch and gave him an appreciative wink, like he had passed muster and was ready to enlist. *Jesus, Phyllis, you've got some brass on you, you horny old bat.*

"I saw you on *The Late Show*. You were terrific."

Here was the boost, welcome and warm. After a solid week of the cocaine drip, no food, and a rainbow assortment of pills, Ronan was squeezed out like an ancient tube of toothpaste. But suddenly he was back from the brink and damn near born again, revived to his former glory by simple, unfiltered praise. It rarely mattered to him coming from friends or family, no matter what that made him for feeling that way. It mattered even less coming from his agent or the critics, who could all take a long walk off a short pier. But when it came from strangers, it filled him, a nourishment almost better than food or sex or drugs.

"Thank you," he said. "That's very kind of you."

She touched him again, leaning over the aisle, trying to get closer to him.

"I mean it. You make me laugh and laugh."

She eyed him, heavy-lidded, an upward glance, a smirk at her lips. The look. If there was one thing he'd never ever in his life get used to, it was the look. An open invitation. *I want you to fuck me.* Plain as day. So simple and direct a feeble-minded farm hand could figure it out. *I will fuck you right here. I will do shit I won't ever do with my husband or boyfriend or significant whatever. You got it right, hot stuff, I will do terrible, terrible things. In fact, let's find a bathroom.* Ronan never thought of a woman's desire as frightening, but the first couple times he got the laser eyes, he was rattled.

He grew up a pimply-faced nobody with big fisheye glasses held together by duct tape half the time after another ass-kicking from small town bullies. He was lanky, with ugly braces stuffed into his mouth, the pure and definitive antithesis of anything women would consider desirable. But age, a little grit, a little California sunshine, and a widening spotlight for his career had opened doors, and legs, that were previously closed tight against him. A spot of LASIK surgery, a personal trainer (once he'd hit Netflix, his agent demanded it), and the California regiment of weird diets and weirder supplements had made him almost pass for handsome. But he still peered out from his new eyes a pimply-faced nobody and his brain still had trouble wrapping itself around women giving *him* the look. Not that he didn't capitalize on it.

"I have my moments," he said.

She reclined in her chair, sighing. She pushed her chest out, almost imperceptibly, and she uncrossed and recrossed her legs, just long enough, just luxuriant enough for him to get a good look at her legs and hitch her skirt up the slightest inch. The offering. Like a sacrifice on a dais to some primitive jungle god. *Ravage me, Tarzan!* Ronan was a nobody four years ago and the only thing that had changed was that his face was on television now. He was still very much the same. In fact he suspected he would always be the same, regardless of his fame or fortune. But the perception around him had changed. He carried an odd status now - what the kids and shrinks called social proof - the golden ticket behind the money, power, and fame that had been greasing wheels since time immemorial. Athletes, musicians, A-listers, hell, even small-time comedians lived in a vastly different world than civilians.

"That bit about running and working out," she laughed. "Oh god, it gets me every time."

That bit had put him on the map. It sent him viral from a ramshackle amateur club in Ohio. He was tanking a set and drunk enough to try something new. Some kids filmed the set and put in on YouTube and one week later, he had over a million views and his first call from an agent. Not bad for a guy who shunned social media like the plague. That bit lifted him out of poverty and anonymity like a sweeping tide.

"I think you're very talented," she added.

He nodded appreciatively and tipped his drink to her. He gazed at her, really looking now, for the LA tell. There was no question she was from there - the clothes, the hair, the shoes, the air about her, down to the accent. If she wasn't from there, she'd sure as hell been out there long enough to be thoroughly assimilated into the churning, single-minded organism that was the Los Angelino. Ronan had learned, to his amusement and sometimes horror, that every single person who resided in the city and surrounding area was completely and deliriously strange. Decidedly strange, in some odd, weird, goofball way that no amount of green goddess smoothies or high colonics at yoga retreats were ever going to take away. Whackjob quirks and real rips in the fabric of psyches were the norm in the valley and while most of the populace were relatively harmless, it paid to know the general flavor of the poison before drinking of it fully.

He scanned down her legs to the red-bottom heels and the Fendi tote, slightly open, revealing a headscarf, long wallet, and the corner of a metal box with an LED panel flashing red numbers on it. Ronan saw, with growing interest and a touch of disquiet, that the numbers on the panel were steadily counting down. She caught him peeking and read his mind an instant later. She laughed broadly and shook her head at him.

"Don't worry!" she said. "It's not a…you know."

She made an exploding motion with her hands and a daffy *Ka-Plew!* noise under her breath that made Ronan grin.

"It's a part of the treatment."

Impossibly, she leaned in even closer across the aisle, clamping a hand around his forearm. She looked up and down the aisle, making sure airline staff were out of earshot.

"Vaginal tightening."

She beamed at him and produced a pink business card from the depths of her bag. She handed it over and waited while Ronan scanned the card.

"Testing a new prototype now," she said and wiggled in her seat. "It's a doozie!"

God, I will always love California, Ronan thought, pocketing the card and turning to her.

"I have questions."

She laughed again, high and bright, and stroked his arm.

"I have answers," she said. "I'm pitching VCs when I land in Boston, so you can be my practice pitch. Is it a deal?"

He smiled at her and reached out to shake her hand.

"Deal."

She held his hand.

"Why are you flying east? Doing a show at the Wilbur?"

He released her and reached for his drink, draining most of it in one good gulp.

God damn you, Dad. You're the only one could ever bring me back. Only you.

He shrugged and set the drink down on the tray.

"Doesn't matter," he said. "I'm your audience. Tell me everything there is to know about tightening up drafty vaginas."

She clapped her hands together and squealed. Drinks were ordered. Prototypes were unveiled. Trade secrets were disclosed. Flight attendants busied themselves around them. The guy next to Ronan continued to sleep, utterly unaffected by the shameless giggling and flirting. Ronan, in parts amused, astonished, and enamored by his new companion, welcomed the fanfare and the distraction, but somewhere underneath still felt the clear pangs of regret and loss as the plane droned closer to the place he once called home.

Chapter Two

Ronan's earliest memory of his father was at the ocean. It was high summer and Ronan was likely three or four at the time. He remembered the smell, surf and sunscreen. He remembered the haze, baking hot and rising up out of the scorching sand, softening the edges of his vision, making each droplet of moisture a prism, reflecting spots and pinprick dazzles of colored light up and down the shore. A day of rainbows.

The sky was pale blue, punctuated with wispy strings of clouds like streamers of cotton or gauze carelessly strewn across the open sky. He remembered his dad, sturdy and strong, holding his hand as they jumped waves near the shore. He had been mesmerized and frightened by the powerful pounding of the waves. The sound of the crash was loud, smashing the shore with white foam and salty spray that rose high into the air. It was the first time he distinctly felt the very adult sensation of being torn. Kids were screaming and jumping in the water, swimming, playing with toys, chasing each other, meticulously constructing castles from the wet sand. Ronan knew it was okay, but he felt hesitance, a pull toward safety, an instinctual resistance to fear.

But his father, mighty and benevolent, trim and strong, overflowing with youth and vigor led him carefully to the water, introducing him by sure and careful inches to this great frothing friend. Ronan flirted with the sea, tapping at it with his toes, feeling himself sink into the warm sand as the waves retreated. As he grew bolder, his father took him out further until he was in just up to his waist. When a wave came to crash he made to retreat, but his father held his hand, tightly, but not unkindly. He smiled down at him, a look Ronan never forgot.

I've got you.

As the wave crashed, Ronan felt incredible strength lift him up and out of the water and there was a sensation like no other, wondrously new and so incredible that he could only shriek with delight. He was flying! The lift and rise was a revelation and he felt a flurry of new emotions, ones so powerful they would forever bond to him, imprinting on his young psyche for a lifetime. Here was a thirst for adventure. Here was a thrill for excitement. Here was the desire to explore, to know, to quest, to move his body, to push his limits and feel the rush of playful exuberance. It was in that blazing afternoon that Ronan fell forever in love with the sea.

His father held him steady and sure, strong like a faithful draft horse that never tired. He must have jumped hundreds of waves, inexhaustible, and his father never left his side or loosened his grip. He held Ronan like a kite string, letting him drift and wander and fly free against the constant rhythm of the waves. Ronan trusted that grip, trusted in absolute safety. He never doubted it, never once feared it would fail him. Jump and lift. Jump and lift. The two of them, inseparable, indomitable, conquerors of the mighty Atlantic.

And now?

Better come quick, Ronan. I don't think he's got much time.

Now the waters had receded. The surf had died down to a listless echo of that blazing summer day. The sun was near to setting and a long night loomed just over the horizon. The sand was dry and crumbling and the water had grown cold. The Pacific was a different animal. It was bluer, deeper, crueler somehow than his memories of the warm green seas of his childhood. Ronan was a different animal too. Far from the boy playing in the waves with his dad, Ronan had receded too. While he knew the strong, protective grip of his father was long absent, he knew acutely that it would soon be gone altogether.

Better come quick.

At 40,000 feet, Ronan finally felt the first bitter sting of grief.

∗ ∗ ∗

Dear Ronan,

My father was a policeman. Did you know that? He used to scream and break things and tune up my mother when he'd had enough to drink. Not that she didn't deserve it half the time. She was no gem, my mum. He never laid a hand on me and he never got the chance to get too weird, but it was coming. I could feel it, like the heavy in the air before a storm. He chased away boys with a shotgun and he'd show me lurid crime scene photos when he was drunk.

"You see!" he'd slur. "See what men are capable of! Get a good look, missy, because this is who they really are!"

Sometimes I'd steal them and hide them under my mattress like a boy hides porno mags. I'd imagine a man - not a boy, not my peers, but a man - who wanted me so badly or loved me so violently that he'd rip me apart with his bare hands. I imagined bleeding for him, my devotion splashed all over the walls, willful, eager, laying myself out for him to savage. Could I do that? Did I possess that kind of power - to drive a man to murder?

I saw them, Ronan. All of them. My uncles, my teachers, even my dad as they started to notice me. My budding, painful breasts. My ass blossoming and legs stretching out of clothing that was all of a sudden too tight in all the wrong places. The Lolita stare. Men were noticing me. My power was growing.

I was a cocktease before I even knew what a cock looked like, smelled like, tasted like. I learned to be like the sun. I didn't have to do anything, I could just beam it out, this deep plea, this ache, a cry for murder. I used to fuck myself to crime scene photos. Twelve years old, humping my pillow, fist jammed into my mouth so I wouldn't cry out, fantasizing about being broken open like a piece of fruit by the calloused hands of a man beyond reason. To be pissed on, shat upon, used and thrown away like a rubber on the floor of a taxicab. I didn't want to be fucked, Ronan, I wanted to be destroyed. Because then? Then I'd live forever.

My father inadvertently turned me into a nymphomaniac. Trying all the ivory tower bullshit to keep me locked away, our home was like a convent. A fortress. He hated that I was born a girl, maybe that I was born at all. He hated that I didn't give a fuck about his attempts to jail me or his 1950s virgin doctrine. He hated me. Do you get it? He HATED me. He'd look at me sometimes and I could feel the fury, the venom, the molten heat of his disgust. I was an only. No brothers, no sisters. Just me and my checked-out mum and this drunken bastard who held us captive and slipped a little further away from himself every day.

He shot himself on a rainy day in March in the garage with his service revolver. I was freshly fifteen. That night I snuck out, hitched into the city, and fucked a nightclub bouncer in his car under a streetlight. I came so hard I broke the guy's seat and when he tried to sweet talk me after, I punched him hard enough to break his nose. He turned then. God, Ronan, he turned. His face, like a mask fell away and there was always a monster underneath. He was blood and teeth, grabbing at me, ready to pull me apart. I laughed in his face and kicked him in that deflating cock of his that had filled my wound so right just moments before.

I ran! I ran into the night, shrieking and laughing: "I did it! I did it! I did it!" I knew for all that he'd put me through, my shitheel of a father had made me into a survivor. As much as he'd ruined me, warped my defiant young brain, he could die knowing that I was just like him. A true predator. They could try and I would tempt them, but I would never be destroyed.

I never went home. I started shooting scenes three years later. The rest, as you know, is history.

The point I'm trying to make, my sweet Ronan, is that your father loves you. He raised you right and he made genuine sacrifices to get you where you are. He fawned over you and tried to instill values and ethics and substance into you. Even when you turned your back on him and all that family quicksand, he still called, he still wrote, he still reached for you because he loves you.

Love is a terrible burden. It's a gift that demands reciprocity. It is a call that cannot go unanswered. The guilt! Jesus Christ, the guilt. It drips and soaks and floods into the cracks of you until, like some poor, sliced-up girl in a crime scene photo, you get cut to ribbons by it. Love is selfish, insecure, needy, and always keeping score. To love someone is to harpoon them. Know this to be true.

The best thing a parent can do for their child is die. Cut the cord, snap the rope, kick the dead man overboard and let the sea do what it will to him. Be free as I am, Ronan. Join me. At last. Be free of attachment and obligation. Plant that corpse in the sour earth and run from that tomb of a town and never look back. Your life only begins when his ends. It is only then that you will be truly free to be yourself. Unfettered. Unburdened. Fucking free.

That's how I want you when you murder me.

Lovingly,

Margot

* * *

"So, I can assume from all this…"

Holly Learner, Founder and CEO of Yoni Holistics squeezed her hand into a fist across the aisle.

"Like a drum."

Ronan coughed and reached for a glass long empty. He could see the city out the window. The man next to him was just coming around. In ten minutes they'd be on the ground.

"Don't take offense," Holly said. "I'm going to do woo here on the way down. I hate flying. See you on the flip."

She closed her eyes and lay her hands, palms up, on her knees, making circles with her thumbs and forefingers. She began to mumble in tongues.

"None taken," Ronan said and started running down the checklist in his mind.

The flight attendant took his glass and some trash from

the rousing man at Ronan's side. Holly was still transcending, head jerks now accompanying her murmurs. The counter on her prototype had finally reached zero. Ronan shook his head to clear it and chased away spots in his vision with a head jerk of his own. When the wheels touched the ground, Ronan felt solidity return to him, muscle memory. It felt a lot like putting on old armor. Boston grew around him, lending him gravity, a heaviness in his legs and hands. He felt himself toughening.

"Our offering was received," Holly told him, as if she landed the plane herself.

Maybe she did.

"Namaste, friend," he replied, hands clasped together, bowing to her.

She collected her bag, frowning at the contraption with the LED panel. She turned on him.

"Kegels, Ronan," she said. "That's the moral of the story."

He nodded solemnly, raising his prayer hands above his head and shaking them at her.

"Blessed be," he said.

The jetway fastened onto the plane and passengers milled around out of their seats.

"How long are you in town?" Holly asked.

He shrugged, shouldering his carry on.

"Not sure," he said. "Kind of playing this one by ear."

She softened, the lines around her mouth smoothing, and then her lips broke apart and Ronan caught something so akin to gentle he had to break eye contact.

"My mom died last year," she said.

Timidly, he met her eyes. She reached out to touch his

sleeve. Her fingers braced him and he felt himself rise to his full height. She retracted her hand and gazed at him, satisfied.

"I'm at the Boston Harbor Hotel," she paused. "Through the weekend."

The cabin door popped open and the first gust of the outside blew in. October. October. October.

There it is.

Ronan breathed deeply, memories unfurling at the scent of it. Fireplaces, crunching leaves, whiskey and cigarettes. Remembering himself, he gestured to the door and Holly stepped out into the aisle. Halfway up the jetway, she turned to look at him over her shoulder.

"You'll be okay."

The kindness braced him further.

"Boston Harbor Hotel," he said.

"Through the weekend."

He tipped Holly a salute as they came out into the terminal. There she was swallowed by a hen-like gathering of young women in matching pale blue pantsuits all trying to talk to her at once. Ronan turned toward baggage claim, taking the escalator down to the revolving carousels. There to greet him, the only person Ronan trusted in all of New England.

"Arlo," he said.

The hand gripped his, tight, and they pulled into an embrace, shoulder to shoulder. Here it was now. Like the brittle snap of a sheet of ice. Definitive. Unmistakable.

Ronan had landed.

Chapter Three

Arlene Rinaldi, Arlo to her friends, gave Ronan the once over and whistled.

"Are we the bug or the windshield today, dear?"

He made a little bow and waved his hand out in a flourish for her.

"Fuck that bug, I'm the windshield." He rose. "At your service."

She grinned.

"You look like you went through the propeller."

He ran a hand down his face and gave her his patented puppy dog look.

"You love me."

"I fear California has crippled you with delusion."

They wandered to the baggage chute. Ronan felt tension lifting as they eased through the crowd. He admired Arlo's long leather trench coat, her combat boots, and her character strut.

"How those Cadillacs selling?"

She turned on him, feline.

"They practically sell themselves," she said. "I meet a lot of little wifeys."

"Bored?" he asked.

"And curious," she said.

"I'll bet."

"I like to ease them in."

He laughed.

"That's a good one."

She flared her coat and stuck an expensive chest out at him.

"When you walk into a Cadillac dealership, you're already going to buy. I just have to put you in the right model."

"California would love you," Ronan said.

She shook her head.

"Boston loves me."

She pointed a finger at him.

"And speaking of love-"

"No," he said and made a point of focusing on the conveyor, searching for his bag.

"What really happened with you and Anna Kendrick?"

"No," he repeated.

"You looked so happy at her premiere."

He put a foot up on the metal rail of the conveyor and leaned over his leg, tuning her out. She produced a cell phone from her jacket pocket, chuckling, and he knew what was coming. She jammed a button and pushed the phone into his face. On the screen, a blonde woman in a torn up wedding dress was enthusiastically servicing a group of naked men.

"Now what could break up the love birds?" she mused. "What could it be?"

People were looking up from their own phones and conversations with a mixture of embarrassment and amusement.

"She's talented. I'll give her that."

He reached for her phone, but she danced away.

"Volume," he pleaded, looking around.

She instead turned up the volume on the phone and taunted him with it.

"What is her name, Ronan?"

He glared at her. She turned up the volume to the maximum and the sounds of porn echoed through baggage claim.

"Say her name and I'll stop."

"Margot," he said.

"Margot?"

He winced and surrendered.

"Margot Throbbie."

Arlo howled, delighted. She threw her head back and cackled, chest heaving. Ronan pounced on her distraction and snatched the phone out of her hand. He silenced it and fumbled, trying to get the clip of his-

(*Friend? Muse? Lover? It was more than nothing, but was it anything?*)

-admirer off the screen. Arlo took her phone back, laughter subsiding into giggles.

"I can't tell you her real name," he defended.

"I do not care," Arlo said. "She will be Margot Throbbie to me for all time and that? Oh goodness, that is priceless."

"It's clever."

"It's something," she said and reached around him towards the conveyor. She snatched his bag up in one smooth movement and tossed it to him. He opened his mouth-

How did you-

"I know you, Ronan. Or I thought I did. Let's go."

He followed her out the doors to baggage claim and into the crisp night outside. She lit a cigarette and passed it to him. He took it from her gratefully. She lit one of her own and they smoked in silence, dodging cabs and luggage carts on the way to the parking garage. When they arrived among the silent rows of cars, he turned on her.

"Your porno name," he said. "Go."

No hesitation. No deliberation. She fired at him.

"Strap-along Cassidy."

He laughed out loud, sputtering smoke in a harsh bark.

"Wow. That's good," he coughed. "That's damned good."

She beamed at him. He caught his breath and shivered as the chill crept down his neck and through his shirtsleeves.

"Cold?"

He rubbed his arms and shrugged her off.

"I have your leather in the car."

He gaped at her.

"You kept it?"

She breathed smoke.

"I figured if you OD'd again, it might be worth something on the open market."

He shook his head.

"I can't believe you kept it."

"Strap-along has you covered."

He laughed again. She pointed to his cigarette.

"Smoke it up, you can't puff in the car."

He flicked the butt away.

"Yes, dear," he said, pausing, looking at her. "Why didn't we ever get married, huh?"

She stopped, dropped her cigarette and crushed it out with her boot heel.

"Because you don't impress me, Ronan," she said. "That's why this has always worked."

She produced a key fob from her jacket and clicked a button. A sharp black Cadillac SUV lit up and growled at them from behind a V-shape grille like a shark's mouth.

"Your chariot awaits," she said and climbed inside.

He followed her, settling in at her side, content to be led for the rest of the evening. She revved the black beast, not without some pride, and punched her way out of the airport. As they came out of the tunnel, she popped the sunroof and the city skyline bloomed before them.

Ten years fell away, whipping out the open roof, consumed by the October sky. Ronan stretched in his seat and allowed himself to feel a sense of peace for the first time in many long weeks. It wouldn't last. It never did.

But it was a fine place to start.

$$* * *$$

Ronan swept his palm across the dash and down into the center console. He ran his hands over the leather at the sides of his thighs and whistled.

"This is a really nice car."

"I can put you in one for eighty-five."

He tapped the glass of his window.

"This monster is worth eighty-five?"

She laughed.

"No," she said. "This monster is worth a lot more than that, but we have to start negotiations somewhere."

He frowned and pointed to the media deck that dominated the dash between them. The station was tuned to an NPR show.

"Politics? Come on."

She clicked a lacquered fingernail against the panel.

"There's a lot going on in the world, dear," she said. "Not a great time to be carrying the double x chromosome, in case you haven't noticed."

"Planning on a visit from the stork anytime soon?" he asked.

"Not the point," she said. "I don't need old white guys up in my business."

"California, Arlo. I'm telling you. Pussy hats as far as they eye can see."

She snorted and laughed without humor.

"Fuck those basic Goop bitches. They do it because it's trendy. Out here we still earn it."

Ronan said nothing, but he waved at the console dismissively.

"Fine," she said and punched a button.

Eddie Murphy came out through the speakers - *Raw*, 1987, red leather suit, goonie-goo-goo all the way down.

"Better?"

He nodded.

"Now, Eddie? Eddie impresses me," she teased.

He remembered being a kid and listening to Eddie Murphy for the first time. On cassette, no less. Old school. *Delirious* and *Raw*. They were making the rounds of his middle school and all the kids were hocking bootlegs.

Not allowed to watch such things on television, Ronan relished the chance to transgress with a singular voice that, along with Robin Williams and George Carlin and SNL, opened a world of humor and defiance that pushed him, even then, to a path that led on stage.

He did a stand up bit for his high school talent show and jumped with both feet into, both statistically and anecdotally, the most useless undergrad major of all time: theater. But even then, Ronan had accepted one thing that helped elevate him among his peers. He was never going to fit in with the world of nine-to-five. Things like accounting, finance, business, and law were like distant planets to him, orbiting so far away from his day-to-day, they were scarcely an afterthought. The idea of being chained to a cubicle was egregious, inhumane if he allowed himself to be dramatic. Whatever came of his wasted time in college and the blurry years right after, a plaque with his vacant smile and dead-eyed mugshot as Employee of the Month was never going to happen.

He cut his teeth in restaurants. It's how he met Arlo and the rest of his once infamous Boston crew. There was something to be said for trauma bonding, Ronan believed, as the closest thing to family outside of his own fractured home came from his friends in the industry. The average person could scarcely fathom the scope of the gritty, promiscuous, booze-addled, and oftentimes hilarious world of the service industry. It was a world that even now, despite his rising station and almost embarrassing financial success, he still missed acutely.

Arlo thumbed towards the back of the truck.

"Your coat is back there somewhere."

He unclipped himself and twisted around, sorting through a pile of clothing on the back seat until his hands found a familiar shape. He retrieved the deep maroon racer from the pile. He held it up and stared at it with nostalgic pride. He was almost afraid to put it on, fearful it wouldn't fit him or that somehow, his style had moved on from those dim, hip days of bar hopping and chasing co-eds. But as he slid it on, it conformed around his body, made for him alone. He stretched his arms through the sleeves and shrugged his shoulders. The creak and rustle of the distressed leather was a homecoming whisper. He immediately felt better, cooler, more in control, armed against barbarians at the gate.

"There he is."

He sighed, passing wordless gratitude to Arlo as she navigated them through the waterfront and closer to the city.

"Where we heading?"

She looked at him, incredulous, like he should absolutely know. When he met her with a blank stare, she goaded.

"It's Thursday."

"Okay-"

"It's fucking *Thursday*, Ronan."

"You know repeating the same thing over and over-"

She turned up her lip.

"Jeez, you're dumb."

"That's a damn dirty lie."

"Where did we always meet on Thursdays?"

Understanding dawned.

"The Green Dragon?"

She winked at him.

"I got you ten minutes. You're the opening act and no one knows except the MC."

"Shit, Arlo, I haven't done an open mic night in..." he paused. "A minute."

She lit a cigarette and cracked her window.

"Better sack up then. You've got a lot of fans in this town."

"I thought you said we couldn't smoke in the new car."

She grinned.

"I said *you* couldn't smoke in the new car."

She blew a cloud into his face.

"I can do whatever I want."

He reached for her cigarette, but she swatted him away, content to tease him all the way to their old stomping ground.

Chapter Four

Ronan loved the smell of bars. The reek of stale beer that had seeped into the floors and walls like a coat of paint. The waves of perfume and cologne and raw, unfiltered hormones that wafted through the air in a collected cloud of desire. The carrion stench of urine and vomit that rose up from the bathrooms. In the old days, smoke, thick and pungent, like mustard gas, stung his eyes, long lingering in his clothes and hair. Under it all, the sweet smell of memory.

Bars were museums, sacred repositories of lost laughter and stolen moments, curators of fisticuffs, fluffy rails of cocaine off the backs of filthy toilets, frenzied fucking in dark corners, and decades of jukebox tunes with floors stomped flat from dancing.

Like women, each was fundamentally the same, yet all were unique and deliciously different, with flavors and secrets to discover, each more revealing than the last. In bars, Ronan triumphed. The beer and liquor went down like water and the volume ratcheted up until his throat was hoarse from shouting and laughing. Dim lighting flattered all who passed through those hallowed halls and cast deep shadows for the lovers, the dealers, and the cockroaches. Bottles and glasses crashed together and the sweating mass of human flesh seethed and gyrated, each drink peeling away inhibition and care like snakes shedding outgrown skins.

And when they knew you? When you became a regular and the staff adopted you and you had *your* seat to hold court like a king of old? That was the X on the treasure map. It was the key to a secret society, the implicit guarantee that you were looked after, cared for, a member of the inner circle. Skipping down travel-worn steps with a nod from the bouncer and past heavy wooden doors to a beautiful bartender in a black tee-shirt and painted-on jeans with your usual cocktail waiting for you on the polished shellac of a bar as strong and sturdy as the beams of a Viking battleship. That was heaven.

Ronan felt the crowd part for him, a ripple of recognition spreading out to the far corners. He breathed deeply, taking in the old, warm, familiar scent that, like a time machine, transported him instantly back to the first night he grabbed a microphone here. They pushed their way up to the bar where a raven-haired bartender with an intricate sleeve tattoo greeted them. Arlo stepped up onto the railing of the bar, leaned over, and kissed the woman, lingering.

"Deirdre, this is Ronan. Ronan wants a boilermaker. Make it two."

Deirdre smiled at Ronan.

"I loved your Netflix special," she said. "It's a real pleasure."

He smiled back.

"Thank you. I love your sleeve."

She held her arm out so he could get a better look. Buddhas and mandalas traced intricate patterns down to her fingers. The artwork was fine indeed.

"The rest of her?" Arlo purred. "Like a Rembrandt."

Deirdre winked at them and turned to make their drinks.

"I didn't know you knew anything about art."

Arlo smirked at him.

"I don't," she said. "But I enjoy collecting masterpieces."

Two shots of whiskey and two barrel sized glasses of Pabst appeared before them. Ronan felt a clenching in his stomach. Three gin and tonics and a rubbery chicken contraption on the plane had been his only sustenance all day. His hangover was stubborn and still clung to him, but he wasn't about to stop now.

"Old school?" he asked.

"Old school," Arlo answered.

They reached for the shot glasses and held them over their beers, poised for destruction.

"Let it be sung, let it be told," he said.

"We never grow up, we never grow old," she finished

They dropped the shots into the beer and reached for them, chugging the cold brew down in great gulps, streams of it running down their chins into the Vs of their necks. Finishing at the same time, they slammed their glasses down on the bar. Ronan burped loudly and Arlo patted the center of her chest with her fist. She circled the empties with her finger and nodded to Deirdre for another round.

Ronan protested weakly, more a token gesture than any real show of resistance. When the next round appeared, he played his part dutifully, knowing then, perhaps more keenly than any other time in the last few years, that the reckless role he had cast himself in was perilously close to permanent. And was there regret there? At last? He honestly couldn't say.

Ronan wiped his face and scanned the crowd. It was thick

and swelling and the bar was loud. The usual mix of college kids, young professionals, and seasoned barflies, unchanged by his years away, congealed around him. This was a laughing crowd, he could tell. He could always tell. They would be generous and they would work for him. He felt the telltale wave of excitement and adrenaline flood through his system.

For all his faults, he never got stage fright. He'd get the hormone dump and a jangle in his nerves, but not like some of his contemporaries. He knew a woman who threw up every time, before and after. He knew a guy who had to be on something or it was a total no-go. He knew too many booze hounds and pill poppers and comics who rehearsed sets to exhaustion, committing to total memorization as the only way to survive under the spotlights. But Ronan, scared sick by pretty much every other social encounter in his life, turned into another man when he stepped before them.

He was a ringmaster, a carnival barker, a whipping lion tamer who slapped and stirred them awake, snapping at them with a wit that rose and fell with sharp cracks, marking them, stinging them, erecting pyramids from the fuel of their glee. For those moments, Ronan lost himself in performance, shrugging off all that made him heavy and sad and slow like a big shaggy dog shaking himself dry after a soaking rain. He sharpened. He lengthened. He unfolded himself, stretching far outside his fleshy cage and reached for something he could only call sublime.

The audience called. Forever and always they called. Ronan was built to answer.

* * *

At 9:07, propped up by boilermakers and the hum of the crowd, fiercely craving cheeseburgers and a greasy plate of French fries, he stepped up to the microphone.

You shouldn't be here.

The voices had been silent for a long time. He'd pushed them down, suppressed them violently with an ever expanding catalogue of drugs, drink, retail therapy, and women. Each time he felt the first whispers crawl over his shoulder and into his ear, he crushed them into oblivion, swimming farther and farther from the shore and into the heavy blue crushes that drowned conscious thought. Margot had been a willing accomplice in his quest for emptiness, supplying him with seduction and sex, surrounding him in sexy outfits, toys, perfumes and oils and edible everything, and a steady stable of nubile friends to play with. She'd given Ronan a crash course in human sexuality that he'd never had the chance to explore when he was just a regular schmo.

It worked, all of it, but it was eroding him. His agent had given him a talking to at their last meeting and not a few of his friends, if there was such a thing in Los Angeles, had warned him that Charlie Sheen was not a role model. Margot had upset the apple cart. The thing with Anna Kendrick was ugly and while she herself was not vindictive, the gossip columns and the tabloids were more than happy to fill in the silences with enough speculation to fuel rumors up and down the coast.

Pornstars are trendy, Ronan, his agent had said as they sipped Negronis on the sundeck of some new bistro down near the studios. *Dating pornstars never will be. Get that distinction straight or we're going to have problems going forward.*

He denied and defended, but he could see, forever seared

into his mind, how precarious fame really was and how everyone in California who flirted with the spotlight stood on a fault line. One big quake and it was over. He saw his world shrinking, his own autonomy and control being taken away from him in tiny bites and percentages. The grim calculus was more and more apparent each day: The more they looked at you, the less room you had for a life of your own. Life under the microscope brought with it pressures he never dreamed of, pressure enough to crush him into dust or a diamond, depending on how he navigated his meteoric rise. It was no wonder the Disney kids all went crazy.

Dip in the pool, honey. No one's saying you can't enjoy yourself, she said. *Just don't drown in it.*

But the voices persisted. For the first time in his life, Ronan marched himself into a psychiatrist's office and walked away with a prescription for Xanax and Lorazepam. Nothing in those bottles did anything that drugs and liquor weren't doing already, but they helped. For a while anyway. Nights were the worst. Those hours between 3am and dawn, he'd come wide awake, soaked in sweat, sheets kicked away, breathing hard, a crushing weight sitting on top of his chest. He'd sit at the side of his bed, holding his temples with both hands or biting his nails to the quick as a Greek chorus cried out, high and clear, with lip-stinging acidity, the songs of his deepest shame.

You shouldn't be here, Ronan. How dare you? You self-centered shitstain. How dare you have a good time while your poor father clings to life. How dare you turn your back on this little nuclear unit that fed you and clothed you and paid for your education. Who are you to follow your dreams? When the rest of us have to slave and toil and sacrifice for the meager scraps of a normal life.

What makes you so fucking special, huh? You think you're better than us? Is that it? Oh no, your shit doesn't stink. Your majesty! Please, let us bow and grovel! Present that perfumed derriere to us and we will bury ourselves so deeply we'll block out the light like a total eclipse of the goddamned sun. You should have come home straight away, you selfish prick. He could die tonight, and don't even try to tell us that you don't know that. You should have come weeks ago, but God forbid we upset the process of the creative genius! God forbid we detract from you running around with an obscene, glamour-chasing slut and submarining your precious career. We know how you're always so busy. We know we're such a terrible burden, a veritable birth defect that holds you back from what passes for perfection in your steadily disintegrating perception of reality. Surely we don't matter under the big torchlights of HOLLYWOOD, do we? Surely we can't be more than a speck of dust, a mote of irritation, on your giant galling ego. How dare we? Isn't that what you want to say to us? How dare we impose on your time and your trust and your love? How dare we pull the creative genius from his all-important work and drag him back down to the six foot hole in the earth where we all end up equal in the end. We are your obligation, Ronan. Such a filthy word, filthier no doubt than that cocksucker's mouth you're running around with. Obligation. Such a heavy word too. Heavy lies the head that wears the crown, isn't that right? You owe us. That's what that means, isn't it? You owe us. That's what you don't want to admit, what you don't want to look at. You can run to the four corners, past California, past Asia, past the blue brutal gravity of the planet itself, all the way to Mars, straddling an Elon Musk rocket like Slim Pickens, but you will never outdistance yourself from us. You can't cut us out. You can't drink or fuck us away. We are yours, Ronan. We belong to you. We are inseparable from you. To annihilate us is to annihilate yourself and despite your adorable stints in rehab, we all know you don't have the balls to blow the back of your head out like red confetti. Like you fucking SHOULD. No Ronan, you will live. This is your curse and the length and breadth of your burden. You will live. Your father will die. You will see him into the cold, hard Autumn soil and he will wilt and wither and rot and you will continue. You will walk on, through hard, wet streets soaked with the relentless rain of all the tears you've caused. And you will carry him. You son of a bitch, you will carry him until the end of your days. Maybe like Oedipus, you'll tear out your eyes. Or stab at your thighs like Portia. Or chew off your own tongue like Hieronimo. Maybe that filthy chamber pot you love so much will bless you with a syphilitic end and your rotten cock and wasted nose will precede your addled mind into some gutter in the very basement of Los Angeles. But your maiming will not save you. Deep into old age, if you even make it that far, when your fingers are gnarled and your spine is twisted beyond recognition and you cry at night from the pain sunk down deep into you like an oil well, you will still carry him. A port wine stain on your very soul, you will carry him. And at your end, your end in poverty, obscurity, and obsolescence, the wretched fingers of Hell will reach up to your spoiled deathbed and they will drag you screaming down to an end you never had a chance in your miserable life of escaping. Only then will you separate from him. Only then will you feel how that heavy burden of holding him around your neck was the last and only thing that kept you remotely human and remotely lovable. And as he goes up and you go down, you will hear his laughter echo down after you, taunting, triumphant, following you down into the heat and flames and the agony that awaits your immortal soul. This is our promise to you, Ronan, a promise most solemn and most sacred: your father will laugh.

Your father will laugh while you burn.

The microphone stinks like cheap beer and the rancid spittle of a thousand hopeful comics who grabbed it with trembling hands. The lights are hot and as soon as Ronan wraps his hands around the plastic and pulls it from its sheath, he feels the power rise inside him. He inhales and grins out at them and already, they are laughing. He dives in with an almost frightening tenacity for his set, throwing himself wholly into a performance that demands so much from him, there is no room for anything else.

For those ten precious minutes, the voices at last fall silent.

Chapter Five

Outside, smoking with Arlo, his phone buzzes in his pocket. His set had been pristine and the comics who followed picked up on his energy and the rest of the night was silly and perfect. His cheeks hurt from smiling and the line of people who'd come up to greet him seemed endless, like a mad receiving line at some dignitary's wedding. *Hello, thank you, nice to meet you. Next!* Now reality, the pesky and impertinent cop at the driver's side window, threatened to bring him down from euphoria.

Anya calling.

Ronan sighed and extricated himself from the small throng gathered around them. He walked towards the lip of an alley and brought the phone up to his ear.

"Hello, sister," he said.

"Hello, brother," Anya said.

Her tone was the same tired and annoyed tone she pretty much always had since the kids were born. But that bode well, it meant things at the hospital hadn't gone sideways, at least not yet. Ronan heard the first bits of anxious chatter rising up in his ears and he shook his head to clear them out.

"What's the report?"

She sighed, hugely resentful at his absence, but too worn out to pick a fight.

"Are you drunk?"

"Nope," he said.

"Where are you? I hear people."

"People inhabit the Earth, Anya."

She sighed again.

"When are you coming home?"

"Tomorrow."

"Do you need me to pick you up at the train station?"

He thought about his hometown rolling up through an Amtrak window, a wholesome little New England postcard town where there was a smile and a wave on every corner and milk was still delivered in glass bottles. The thought sickened him and he saw himself trapped there, at the mercy of his sister and grounded without a car to escape.

"I might rent a car and drive down."

"You might?" she asked, voice tight. "Are you going to or not?"

"Look, relax, I'll get there on my own. Now what's the report?"

"I've been praying," she said.

Ronan laughed, he couldn't help it.

"How's that been working out for you?"

He could feel his sister's assuredly un-Christian rage seething through the phone.

"Come right to the hospital when you get here."

"You want me to bring anyth-"

"Goodnight Ronan," she said and hung up.

He stared at his phone for a long minute, lost in thought.

What was it she always said when things weren't going her way? *Lord graciously hear me.*

Lord graciously hear me, he thought. *You're a mean old bastard. You demand worship and obedience and you never give anything in return. You just take and take.*

Of course, Anya's bible thumping didn't happen overnight. Did it ever? It was Matilda that broke her - broke all of them. The sister unspoken, the baby, perfect and bright and gold as rolling wheat fields under a summer sun. She had the best laugh, the ultimate laugh, Ronan's favorite out of the thousands he'd heard on stage. Free from constraint or boundaries, her laughter filled a room and drove out dusty sadness with pure, innocent joy. Tildie, who lit up their whole house and followed Ronan around like a lovestruck puppy dog wherever he went. She'd crawl out of her crib when she was little (*She's an escape artist, that one*, his mother had said) and curl up in bed with him, a soft, strawberry smelling ball of warmth, tiny ringlet curls tickling his nose as she slept. He loved her. Mighty. With all of his heart.

All the while cancer lurked, hidden, mutating and separating in the deep gullies of her bones, taking root and stretching through her golden form, steadily dismantling her from the inside. It didn't last long, thankfully, but it lasted long enough (*It hurts! Ronan, it hurts!*) to ground their happiness into a fine powder that blew away on a warm Spring morning as a small and awful white casket was interred forever beyond their reach. What had Robert Frost said?

So dawn goes down to day. Nothing gold can stay.

Anya had shown up to Tildie's first chemo treatment with a beat up bible she'd dug up from one hidey hole or another, face drawn and serious. She dragged it around the same way she'd dragged dolls around not so long before. Big sister protector with the good book, channeling God almighty himself to show mercy on his humble servants. Anya began demanding Grace before every meal and he'd caught her praying at the foot of her bed most nights, murmuring earnestly to that invisible benevolence.

"Bless momma and daddy and Ronan," she'd whisper. "And please take away Tildie's pain."

She never asked God to take away the cancer though. Even as a child, she must have known somehow that some things were beyond saving. But she asked to take away her sister's pain and that touched Ronan down to his core. It was even sweeter somehow, even more endearing than asking for the obvious. She knew God wasn't a genie in a bottle, at least she knew that. But if He could provide some modicum of comfort, well she'd pray for that all night long.

She prays for you the same way, you know?

He knew. Just as he knew he too was beyond saving. There would be no burning bush outside his window, of that he was certain. But she'd pray to take his pain away. With the same urgent longing and sincerity, she'd put her hands together and wish him the simple charity of a moment without agony. Couldn't he at least do the same for her? Shame burned his cheeks because he knew he could not.

Arlo broke from the crowd and sidled up next to him, sensing storm clouds.

"Everything okay?"

He put his phone away and nodded, suddenly very tired.

"Your dad?"

"He's hanging on."

"And how is the Mother Superior these days?"

"Don't."

"You know all she really needs is a good-"

"Cut the shit, will you?" he snapped.

She took a step back and bowed her head to him respectfully, about the closest thing to an apology he could ever expect from Arlene Rinaldi. His stomach rumbled loudly in the silence and she touched his arm.

"Jesus, you must be starving," she said, defusing him with expert hands. "You wanna get out of here?"

He nodded gratefully, made to leave the alley, and then found himself reaching for her, pulling her to him and embracing her, holding her tightly to him so he could feel the beating of her heart underneath her clothing. She stiffened at first, affection like a foreign language that was always met with suspicion and resistance before understanding. But she found herself softening in his arms and she reached around to embrace him.

They stood hugging in the alley for a long time, warm against the chill, each sending silent prayers to the other that they should know a night without pain.

* * *

Arlo stared at him while he wolfed down his second cheeseburger, pausing only to chug soda or swab a handful of fries through ketchup. She was picking at a garden salad without much enthusiasm, stealing sips of his soda while he stuffed his face.

"What?" he asked, muffled through a mouthful of food.

She shook her head.

"What?" he repeated, taking his soda back from her.

She waved at the remains of feast on the table.

"I'm pretty sure this isn't keto," she teased.

It wasn't quite what she wanted to ask, but it would branch the conversation enough for her to work up the courage to get there. He laughed and stuffed a wad of fries into his mouth with a flourish.

"Damn right it's not," he said. "Those bird beak diets are half the reason the world's gone crazy. Everyone is fucking starving."

She speared an errant tomato and twirled it around her plate.

"Won't your trainer get on your case?"

He laughed again.

"Mitchell? Please. He eats worse than I do."

"Isn't he the guy who got Thor ready for his movie?"

Ronan nodded.

"You know I met him once, Hemsworth. Nice guy. Funny as hell. Built like a brick shithouse."

"God, that man makes me rethink my vagitarian ways."

"Fuck," he said. "Me too, I think."

She stared at him.

"What?" he demanded. "Out with it."

She breathed in and pushed her salad plate away, leaning over the table on her elbows.

"Are you okay, Ronan?"

Band-Aid ripped, plain as day. Arlo wasn't one to mince words.

"Is this because I hugged you?"

"Yes," she said, then hesitated. "No. I don't know."

He batted his eyes at her.

"Arlene, are you worried about me? I'm touched."

She narrowed her eyes.

"Call me Arlene again and there's going to be two funerals back to back."

He passed his soda over to her as a peace offering. She took it and drained it in one gulp, returning the empty cup to him with an arched eyebrow.

"You know that cat poster where the kitten is barely hanging onto the branch and has that fuck-me-running look on its face?"

"Hang in there!" she shouted.

"Yeah," he said. "That's about where I'm at right now."

She frowned at him.

"I'm not real good at the warm and fuzzies, all right. I'm your ride or die, Ronan, don't ever doubt it, but I don't really do pep talks."

"No shit!" he joked, feigning exasperation.

"Fuck you," she said darkly.

He reached for her but she pulled away, crossing her arms over her chest.

"I'm trying to tell you I'm sorry about your dad, you asshole."

He put his hands palm up on the table and looked up towards the ceiling.

"I can't get out of this one, Arlo. Not this time. It's face the music here. Between us girls, I'd rather have cancer in my asshole than set foot in that fucking town again. But here we are."

He leveled a finger at her.

"But you, my friend, have single-handedly made this whole jaunt a *lot* more bearable. The airport pickup, the set at the Dragon-"

He rubbed the sleeves of his old jacket.

"-and this set of beautiful armor, lovingly kept after all these years."

She turned away from him, staring into the crowd of diners, embarrassed.

"I'm trying to say thank you, you asshole."

She turned back to him, softening the slightest bit, but said nothing.

"Gee, you're welcome, Ronan," he said. "I live to serve."

"Lets go smoke," she said at last, picking up a greasy cheese-burger wrapper and throwing it at him.

Sated, slightly unsteady, he rose to follow her out.

"You're welcome, Ronan," she said, barely above a whisper.

He never heard her. Sometimes even the fiercest of love gets lost among words.

* * *

They lingered under a streetlight, chain-smoking, leaned against the solid black bulk of Arlo's Cadillac.

"You can crash on the pullout if you don't want to deal with a hotel."

He rubbed his lower back, wincing, memories of too many nights passed out on Arlo's couch and waking up half crippled rushing back to him. There weren't enough pills in his bag to pay that tab.

"As much as I appreciate the hospitality," he said. "I have a date."

She perked up. He handed the pink business card her way. She took it, nodding.

"Ah, so this is what your set was all about tonight?"

He grinned, boyish, pleased with himself.

"I expect a full report in the morning," she said.

"And you? What's in store for the rest of your evening?"

Arlo glanced at her watch, it was well after midnight.

"I think I'm going to go fetch Deirdre from the Dragon and do unspeakable things to her."

"Strap-along strikes again."

She took first position and curtsied for him.

"You need a ride somewhere?"

He shook his head.

"I think you've done enough for me tonight, Arlo. I'll hop a cab from here. Go get your masterpiece."

He tapped his lips with his forefinger, deliberating.

"What?"

"I do need a favor though."

She narrowed her eyes.

"Okay."

"Are you working tomorrow?"

"Weekends are where the money is, dear, you know that."

"I find myself in need of a car."

She gaped at him.

"Are you serious right now?"

"Can you put me in something sexy?"

"You're actually serious?" she asked, voice rising.

"I'd rather give my money to you."

"Be careful what you wish for, mommy likes nice things."

"Are we doing this?"

"I don't know, are we doing this?"

He nodded, decision made.

"You're fucking crazy," she said. "You know this, right?"

He shrugged, this was not anything he hadn't heard before. He open the back door and fished his bag out of the back. She walked with him to the curb and he put his hand out to flag a taxi down. The night was still busy, but one rolled right up and Ronan got in, tossing his things inside. He thumbed down the window.

"I'll see you tomorrow then?"

She looked at him.

"What?"

She leaned in through the open window and kissed his cheek.

"I take it back," she said.

"Oh yeah? What's that?"

"You," she said. "You're finally starting to impress me."

She pounded on the roof of the cab and it pulled away, merging into traffic, swallowed up in the parade of headlights on Congress Street. Arlo dawdled on the curb, smoking, worrying after her friend and thinking about cat posters as she made her way back to her car.

Hang in there, Ronan. You've still got a lot of fans in this town.

Chapter Six

By noon the next day, Ronan was flying down I-95 in a jet black CTX coupe, putting the turbocharged V8 through its paces. The radio howled AC/DC and wind rushed through the open sunroof, ruffling his hair as he banged his hands on the steering wheel and screeched out lyrics into the cabin. The stickers were still attached to the passenger side window and he hadn't even bothered to take off the paper courtesy mats resting over the real ones on the floor. All that was for later. For now he was enjoying the unparalleled satisfaction of an authentically frivolous expense he'd never have been able to manage not so long ago.

Ronan had never been smart with money. When he had it, he burned through it and when he didn't, he'd learned from the lean years after college that a bag of rice and bowls of ramen went a long way, with a peanut butter and jelly sandwich thrown in here and there for variety. His mother and father had lectured him, relentlessly, about estate planning (*Save 20% of every check, Ronan, and put it in a Roth IRA and leave it the hell alone!*) and the importance of investing. Compound interest. Rah rah. It fell on deaf ears.

He'd worked in restaurants all his life, deviating for a couple of temp gigs at offices, a pitiful stab at manual labor, and odd jobs of questionable legality along the way. He learned to live cheaply and modestly, skipping the trappings so many of his peers fell into with the expensive McMansions and the bling. His meager earnings fit his lifestyle in an odd way - the struggling artist, starving and pinching pennies because there was a larger calling that miraculously managed to take care of him.

Working in restaurants was easy enough and the money ranged from pretty good to half decent. The problem for Ronan was that it was that he was largely paid in cash. Tips were split at the end of the night and after a cut to the house, the bar, and the bussers, he'd walk with a fat wad of cash just about burning a hole in his pocket. His walks would more often than not take him straight to the bar after work to drink with his compatriots and decompress after another night of dealing with the public-at-large. Most nights he'd close the bar and some nights the bartenders would lock the doors and the restaurant crew would stay on, drinking until dawn and tossing new money around with careless ease.

He'd waited tables in so many places in Boston and LA in the beginning that he knew most of the managers and owners and they treated him like family. He ate out constantly, enjoying discounts on food and drink at the places he frequented. When he levied out generous tips to his friends in the industry, it came out to almost what he'd pay if he went out and didn't know a soul. So it really wasn't saving, even with comped meals, was it? It just appeared like saving and Ronan could feel that front pocket growing lighter and lighter each day.

The beat up Ford Focus he'd scarcely made it to LA in was on its last legs, but it still kept humming. He'd found a good mechanic who loved a challenge among all the detailing places south of the city and his old girl still had a few surprises left in her. He loved that car, fawned over it like a pet, and spent whatever money he had left keeping it on life support. He rented a cheap house when he arrived and even when his regular checks started showing four and then five zeroes, he resisted calls to hi-rise lofts or sprawling estates in the hills where keeping up with the pool alone cost more than his rent.

He remembered the first time he bought a suit - a real suit. His agent told him he was going to be on Late Night and, after the initial shock and pinch-me-I'm-dreaming unreality of it passed, he realized he didn't own a single professional thing to wear. Sure, he wore a monkey suit with an apron and ties for work, but they were clip-on ties and he went through white dress shirts the way some of the big time directors went through ingenues.

So he marched himself down to a proper atelier and got himself measured and fitted. A suit was made for him, bespoke in every way, down to the lining of the jacket. He balked at the price tag - it was more than he paid for the Focus in its heyday. He remembered getting off the line with the tailor and pacing up and down the hall of his house, tapping the end of his phone against his teeth, the old anxiety of scarcity gnawing at his guts. All this money on a set of clothing! It was preposterous. What if he couldn't make it back - Christ that was a couple months rent at least. What if he spilled shit on it or got it all snagged up on an errant nail somewhere? With his luck he'd sit in wet paint and there would go six grand. He could wax his shitty beat up Focus with his spiffy new Brioni dishrag.

But he bought it in the end, justifying the purchase right up until he reluctantly handed over his credit card (having practically begged his card company for a temporary credit increase the day before) with the fact that he was going on Late Night. It was Late Night for Christ's sake! The home of David Letterman, Conan O'Brien, and Jimmy Fallon. How many times was a guy ever going to be on Late Night? How many were going to be on it at all? No one in his family, none of his friends, and only a couple of comics he'd met and certainly didn't know well enough to even call colleagues, much less friends.

Something clicked in Ronan when he put the suit on. It was like two heavy gears that had been spinning freely on their own had finally shifted their positions, teeth enmeshed, and were now spinning together. The click was almost audible, as soon as he'd fitted his tie and stepped before the three way mirror in the shop. For whatever his anxiety and his inner Greek chorus of derision taunted him with, he was pimply-face nobody no longer. Despite all worries to the contrary, Ronan looked like a million bucks.

He marveled at himself, almost unwilling to believe it was really him looking back from the mirror. He looked dashing, elegant, like something out of a magazine shoot. He felt taller and stronger and devilish in the most seductive way. He looked serious, a man to be reckoned with, someone important, someone far outside of his day-to-day character. With a wry grin, Ronan realized he looked a lot like his father.

He would go on to bomb with Jimmy Fallon. He'd partied too hard the night before and tried to recorrect the see-saw with uppers the next day and he was sweating and strung out by the time he got to the green room. The crowd was tough like an old Catholic school nun and his jokes just fell out from under him, clattering the floor amid tepid applause and canned laughter. Fallon (perhaps the nicest person Ronan had met in Hollywood to date) tried to save him, but it was bad night and Ronan was certain it was the end of his career when it was over.

God dammit at least I looked good! he said to the cabbie on his way to a bar afterward to drown his misery.

The suit hung for many weeks after that night, dry cleaned after its one night under the lights and protected like a mummy, wrapped in its plastic garment bag in the dry tomb of Ronan's closet. The hit to his career had not been the grim end he feared and it put him on alert. He'd been diligently writing new material, even seeing the beginnings of what could be a special if he could tie it all into a coherent thread. His name was appearing on billboards all over town and almost every night he was on stage with a newfound ease that surprised him.

It got easier to fork over the credit card. He didn't know if it would ever truly be easy, but it was easier. The fear of money and the fear of spending were lessening. The blocks he'd built around being worthy were coming down. In their place was a weird new sensation of enjoyment - pleasure for pleasure's sake. He promised himself he'd never be like the musicians or the athletes, who might as well set their cash on fire for all the bullshit they wasted money on. He wasn't going to end up broke in five years like so many of the washed up has-beens who were now hocking used cars or begging to be in another terrible Hallmark Christmas movie.

The Caddy was a big one though. Flying First Class and power lunches at Melisse were one thing, but dropping what he dropped on this gas guzzling bullet of a car was a stretch. Chock it up to impulse, grief, or decades of scrimping and going without while his friends sent postcards from Bora Bora, he guessed. Maybe all of the above. It didn't matter now. The title was sitting in the glove compartment and for better or worse, his name was on it.

I did it, Dad. Can you believe it? Your misfit kid made good in the end.

"Hell, maybe I'll even bust you out of the ward and take you for a drive."

Subtly, so imperceptible that he didn't even notice, Ronan's foot pushed down harder on the gas pedal and he drove that much faster towards the hospital.

* * *

Ronan hated hospitals. He understood this feeling was potentially universal, but Matilda had driven it home for him. He couldn't fathom how people worked there. He got it about vocations and callings and medical families with long dynasties and names on plaques, but he wanted as much distance between him and these death camps as he could get. How people could spend their lives working with the sick and the dying made no sense. To get up each and every day and march into these chaos wards to fight an unwinnable war against an entrenched and timeless enemy was too much to think about. It sickened him so much he couldn't even muster respect or admiration for their dedication and hard work.

To Ronan it was like being proud of the meat for throwing itself into the grinder. For healthcare workers, he could only muster the dimmest beginnings of pity and a sorrow that ran deep deep in his heart.

As much as he loved the smell of bars, the smell of hospitals made him queasy. The antiseptic overlay with undertones of piss and sickness and the desperation of the sick and dying. It was a rank bouquet that made his nostrils burn. Cheap cafeteria food and the cloying stink of cheap flowers. Unwashed flesh and the reek of leaking fluids. And grief, spreading out over everything like mold or mildew. It was a thick and putrid smell that lay at the very bottom of all the other assaults. It ran up the walls and down the floors, seeping into the crevices, the bedding, even the steel beams that held these pain palaces aloft. It was the smell of endless tears, countless loss, and the wretched whimpers of sorrow.

I can't do this.

But he was doing it. He pushed the voices down and marched through the double doors of the ICU. The security guard gave him a look from his chair and made to get up to stop him, but Ronan glared at him and strode past. An old, jaundiced-looking woman in a dirty pink bathrobe was being wheeled down the hall opposite him. She reached for him, but he strode past her as well. The nurses at the station were all huddled around a television and didn't even look up as he moved on down the hall. He punched the button at the elevator and waited with growing irritation for the doors to open.

By the time he got off at his father's floor, he was practically seething. How could his dad have ended up in a place like this? Was he going to die here? Among these wilting plants that passed for patients? In this godawful stench of fear and hopelessness? He wouldn't allow it. Surely something could be done? Surely they could take him home and get a home care nurse or hospice? He could afford it. He'd gladly pay. Anything, Jesus, anything but Matilda all over again.

I have to get out of here. Please God, you have to get me out of here!

But rage drove him on. Fists balled up at his sides, mouth tight and frowning, breathing in harsh pants, he made his way to the end of the hall. He could feel his heart clench and sweat bead at his forehead, running down the small of his back. He felt a copper taste spread through his mouth and his vision drew down, tunneling until he could only see the floor of the hallway. At the end of the hall - room 627 - he stopped.

He bent over, putting his hands over his knees, and stayed stooped like that for a good minute, drawing in deep breaths and steeling himself for what lay beyond the threshold. It would be Anya and his mother, maybe the kids. God knew who else, probably some sanctimonious priest all too eager to give last rights and get back to the golf course if he knew his sister.

Fuck, maybe it'll be a brass band! Can we please go now? Ronan - please!

He took a swallow of air and pushed the heavy door inward.

* * *

His first thought was confusion. There was no one here. Not his mother, not his sister. The room was empty except for the shriveled lump on a bed, hooked up to softly beeping machinery and the steady rise and fall of a respirator. His second thought was that he'd made a mistake. This was the wrong room. The lump under the pile of blankets was tiny, shriveled up like a prune and skeletally thin. The cheeks were sunken, bones protruding loudly, and white hair sprung up in errant tufts from the top of a liver spotted skull with the skin stretched tight around it. The intubation tube dominated his face, an insult, an ungracious hose jammed down into the tender flesh of his throat. This couldn't be his father. He was in the wrong room. This was-

You've been gone too long, Ronan.

He shook his head to deny the thought purchase and was about to storm out of the room to check the name on the door when his eyes fell on the man's hands. His father's class ring, a treasured memento from Columbia Law School, a ring Ronan had only seen off his hand twice, gleamed out from the edge of a blue blanket. Always worn on the ring finger of his right hand, it was now on the index finger, the others too small and too skinny to allow it anywhere else.

You've been gone too long.

"Oh Dad," he said softly. "What did they do to you?"

He felt his knees buckle and he grabbed out for the railing of the bed to steady himself. He felt a shudder run through him and his stomach flipped. This wasn't happening. This couldn't be real. He was still on the plane, fast asleep and dreaming this whole, horrible nightmare. Very far away from himself, moving automatically and entirely beyond his control, he reached his hand out.

This is not my father.

But it was. As his hand touched the man's hand and he wrapped his fingers around the feverish flesh, he knew. He would know that touch anywhere on Earth. The same hand that held him as they jumped waves all those years ago, now weak and limp and unresponsive to his grip. Ronan felt the first tears spill, wetting the blanket, blurring his vision. He put his free hand to his mouth to choke down a sob. Then he rose and again with that sense of being completely outside of himself, he backed away from the bed.

I can't.

He continued to back away, his rear end colliding with the bed table, sending a cup of ice chips and a pitcher of water and some glasses crashing to the floor. The sound frightened him and he cried out. He turned, tearing open the door and rushed out into the hallway. He lurched down the hall, bouncing off the walls, wiping at his tears with his sleeve. He saw his mother and his sister coming down the hall, laden with food from the cafeteria, but he was running by then.

"Ronan!" they called after him, but he was bolting past the nurse's station and the elevators, racing for the fire stairs as fast as he could. He ran down them and slammed the big metal door to the outside and a whoosh of cold air hit him all at once. He took a deep breath and then he was vomiting into a row of hedges behind the rear hospital entrance. He emptied his guts, heaving and shaking with rage and shame and underneath it all, the stinging betrayal of time.

Chapter Seven

It is 1941 and Arthur Alexander Besso is born, the second of five children, two boys and three girls. He is bawling, squinting and screaming at the light of a new dawn. His mother and father, Italian immigrants from Calabria, bundle him in love and bring him home to begin a new life. Almost a month to the day of his birth, the Japanese bomb Pearl Harbor and the American war machine heaves itself onto the world stage. Arthur remains blissfully unaware.

It is 1948 and Arthur has gone to court with his father, a federal judge on the 11th circuit court in Manhattan. It is the first time he has ever seen a courtroom and he is taken with the pomp and circumstance and regal severity of the proceedings. He marvels at the suits and ties, the rousing oratory of arguments, and the many moving parts of laws that define how he and his fellows must operate in a civil society. He senses a backbone in these halls, the very spine from which all that is good and just will hang. It is the first time he will fall in love with the law. It is a love he will hold for a lifetime.

It is 1957 and Arthur's father suffers a massive heart attack leaning down to pick up the morning paper from the stoop of their brownstone on a random Wednesday. He leaves Arthur his law library and a generous inheritance that will ensure his college and law education continue uninterrupted. He also leaves him a plaque that once hung in his study. *Lus est ars boni et aequi*: The law is the art of goodness and equity. For Arthur, this plaque sums up the entirety of his father's life. He vows at his funeral to honor this.

It is 1960. Arthur listens to Elvis Presley and passes a joint around a circle gathered for a reading of Allen Ginsburg's "Howl". His hair is long and he feels the surge of a new era of possibility dawning on the horizon. He has been reading "obscene" materials and worrying over the first winds of a budding conflict in southeast Asia. He is dating a free spirited, slightly silly girl who tries to charm him away from his studies and though he fights her and ultimately leaves her, she instills in him a sense of social justice and human rights that he will carry into every facet of his future career.

It is 1963 and he is accepted to Columbia Law School. He remembers working harder than he ever worked before, poring over books about torts and civil procedures and sifting through endless piles of case law. He writes until his hand is sore and cramped and his eyes are dry and bloodshot. His hair grays and recedes from his hairline and he develops the first of the ulcers that will plague him his entire life. The demands on him are unparalleled and sometimes at night, he dreams of the hippie girl who loved him and wonders what ever became of her.

It is 1966 and he is clerking for a judge in the lower district courts of Manhattan. The judge is a bastard, with a ferocious temper and a penchant for young legal secretaries. He punishes Arthur for his heritage - *Fucking dagos think this city owes them something! Fucking wops think they run this town. Guinea sluts are only happy on their backs, Arthur, don't you ever forget it.* Arthur learns to work through it, to muscle through the politics and produce powerful and consistently superior work. He meets a lovely woman named Katherine in the legal secretary pool. She laughs at his jokes and he starts taking her to lunch. When he leaves his clerkship, he takes her with him. It is the single best decision of his life.

It is 1969 and they are in a panic. The letter. *You are hereby directed to present yourself for Armed Forces Physical Examination to the local board named above.* In fine physical shape and long past qualifying for an educational deferment, the two are up late into the night arguing over what to do. His colleagues have told him a marriage deferment isn't enough to keep him out and unless they light out for Canada, he will most likely be going to Vietnam. Arthur prepares himself as best he can and for a long time, things are harder than they ever will be again. In the summer of 1969, grimly preparing himself for Parris Island, Katherine tells him, grinning ear to ear, that he's going to be a father. The military rescinds his conscription. His son, Ronan, is born in the Spring of 1970.

It is 1972 and Anya is born. She is silent and serious and looks out at them with watchful green eyes, an old soul from the very beginning. She is the complement to Ronan's mercurial antics and a decision is made. The city is changing. Crime is rising and the whole five boroughs feel like a pressure cooker. This is a different decade, more severe than the last, the final delicate streamers of that wishful Woodstock unity are blowing away, leaving a different America, exposed like the empty socket where a rotting tooth has finally come loose.

They are looking at houses in New England and Arthur is going through the calculations of whether he can make a small private practice work. It is a leap of faith for a family that is hugely risk averse. While a part of Arthur will always miss the warp and woof of the city, he goes willingly into this new chapter of his life.

It is 1976. With a thriving practice and a happy family, the Bessos welcome Matilda into the world. She is a preemie, so tiny and pink and delicate, the children fear to hold her. But when the first laugh spills out of her, it is buoyant and gleeful and loud and their small house finally feels like a home.

It is 1987 and Arthur is numb. Wasted by long nights in the hospital and the hypervigilance of constant emergency, he is a shell of himself. The laugh that warmed up their house is gone. Like the beacon of a lighthouse that has gone out, there is no guide left to save his ship from wreckage. He longs to crash, to dash his heavy hull against the jagged rocks and to drown in the freezing waves, sinking down into the abyss where not even grief can follow him down. He doesn't believe he will cry when they lower the coffin. He has cried so much in the last three years he is certain he must be dried up and barren. But the tears come just the same, copious and ugly, the only response to the wound of his broken heart.

It is 1999 and Arthur feels a swelling inside of him that he never expected to feel again as he looks down at the squirming center of life that is his first grandchild. He knows he will never let Matilda go, he knows she goes with him wherever he travels - the scars are permanent. But he feels he can breathe again and that light and love and the laughter of children have finally returned. He feels this again in 2001 and 2004 at the birth of his second and third grandchild and he is secretly certain (something he will never tell his wife) that three is truly a magic number.

It is 2008 and he is downstairs staring at the microwave. It is late and Katherine has gone to bed. He is up doing work at the kitchen table when his stomach growls. He roots through the fridge, rifling through leftovers until he finds a Tupperware container of his wife's lasagna. He pops the lid and sticks it in the machine. But now that the door is closed, he puzzles over the buttons. He twists his bottom lip between his thumb and forefinger and feels an eerie blankness surround him. He can't remember what comes next. He's used this contraption a thousand times, so much he's never really had to think about it at all. But here he stands, dark looming outside the windows from his lighted oasis in the kitchen, empty of a simple knowledge he has taken for granted. He isn't worried then. He has been working too hard and they've been talking about a vacation for many months, even stepping away from his practice for a couple days a week. But he is troubled. He eats the lasagna cold at the counter, staring at the microwave, struggling to remember how it works.

It is 2010 and it is dark on the highway. Arthur is returning from somewhere, he can't remember where. He is suddenly behind the wheel of a foreign machine that is moving fast enough to frighten him badly. He swerves, uncertain what to do next, and the car lurches into the next lane, just missing the front bumper of another car. A horn honks loudly and panic takes him. He slams the pedals at his feet and the car accelerates and then brakes in violent jerks. He paws at buttons on the console, and fiddles with dials on the sticks coming out of the wheel. He bounces off a guardrail with a terrific squeal and enough of him comes forward and takes control and he finally coasts to a stop in the breakdown lane. He sits there for almost an hour before a state trooper pulls over to check on him. He laughs it off and sends the officer away, fully returned to his faculties and blaming the entire incident on overwork and stress. He never tells a soul what happened.

It is 2011 and he is being honored by the town's Chamber of Commerce at their annual dinner. He finds himself suddenly under a glaring light, looking out at shadowed faces, staring up at him expectantly. There is nervous laughter as the silence stretches. He is holding onto a small pile of note cards. There is writing on them, but he doesn't recognize it. It looks like hieroglyphs. Is this his writing? Are they waiting on him? He feels a pressure in his mind, like a stuck gear grinding stubbornly against its housing. The pressure builds and he feels an old fear reach around his guts. Just as quickly, the gear clicks and he's back. He smiles out at the crowd and delivers his speech to generous laughter and applause. The night continues without incident, but Katherine watches him with new eyes.

It is 2012 and he is fighting with his son. It is a tired argument, worn into deep grooves between them. He is a foolish boy, a romantic, sensitive soul who won't put down the toys of his childhood. He needs to grow up, to accept responsibility, and to shit or get off the pot when it comes to his future. All that talent, all that intelligence, all the wasted potential of a boy who won't step down off the stage and into the stiff, straight shoulders of a grownup. It is a heated argument, both of them shouting, both of them mean-spirited.

Things are said they will both come to regret later and Arthur shows him a touch of cruelty he never expected to use with his only son. Ronan storms off. Three days later, he tells them he's leaving for California. Arthur screams inside to stop him, to pull him into his arms and stop him from leaving. But he says nothing. He knows boys are meant to leave. Every father must face this goodbye. It is the wish of every father to see his son go out and make it in the world, to forge a world of their own, out from the shadow of their parents. But it breaks him just the same. The last time he sees his son, he will be walking away. It is Arthur's most savage regret.

It is 2014 and he is watching his son joke around with Jimmy Fallon on Late Night on channel 12. He marvels at how handsome he is, tanned and sparkling, grinning out at the crowd with perfect white teeth. He feels the first tears at his eyes, then a lump in his throat, and then he's holding Katherine to him and sobbing. *I'm so proud*, he says. *I'm so proud of him.* She holds him and for the first time, allows herself to be worried about something that isn't phantom terror or jumping at shadows. Finally, she is afraid of something all too real.

It is 2015 and Arthur is having trouble reading and completing sentences. Names and dates have been slipping, but he's been able to cover. He is confused a lot these days and finds himself wandering into rooms without knowing why or holding things and not remembering where they came from. Katherine makes an appointment with a neurologist and drags him kicking and screaming into a sterile beige office. A PET scan and cerebrospinal fluid analysis confirm Katherine's terror. Arthur is crushed by the weight of it and the children are devastated. Two weeks later, they revoke his drivers license. One month after that, in the most painful decision of his long and storied career, Arthur officially retires from the practice of law.

It is 2016 and Arthur misses his son. He manages to pull up the FaceTime his grandkids have explained to him a hundred times over and makes the call. A strange man answers, smiling at him in a familiar way. Who is this man? Where is his son? This man is older. Different. It must be a wrong number. This man looks like him, even speaks with the same tenor, but it can't be Ronan. Ronan is still in college, barely a man. Arthur is frightened by this man calling him Dad. This isn't right. Where is his son? He hangs up the phone in a hurry and cries for what feels like hours.

It is 2018 and there is a fire. The kitchen is filled with smoke and a woman is screaming at him. He is doing something, isn't he? Making a pot of tea on the burner? Maybe a bite to eat? There is a black mess of something at the bottom of a scorched frying pan. The burner is high and grease has caught the range on fire. The woman pushes him aside and sprays the countertop with spray from a white extinguisher. She turns on him, furious, and he is afraid. *You almost burned the goddamned house down, Arthur! What were you thinking?* He shrinks, knees folding. He backs away from the yelling woman, her face twisted into a mask of rage. Why is she yelling? Why is she yelling at him? What has he done to make her so angry? His eyes burn with smoke and an alarm is screaming from somewhere overhead. He curls into a ball in the corner of the kitchen, hugging his knees, face buried in the crevice, and he cries and cries.

It is 2020 and he suspects the woman feeding him his breakfast is stealing from him. She is a home health nurse, her name is Beverly (in actuality it is Bethany; Beverly is the name of one of his sisters) and she's come in to help around the house so Katherine can try and get some sanity back in her life. After the fire, adding Beverly was non-negotiable. But she smells off and she has shifty eyes, making too much of a thing about admiring their home. Arthur doesn't like her and swears at her or tries to hide from her whenever she comes over. On a cold day in February, while she's giving him the last of his egg whites, he hits her. There is shouting, yelling, and a tearful exchange with (*Chrissy? Katie? Kay?*) the woman who shares his bed. But he's already forgotten it and eager to see if Johnny Carson is on.

It is 2021. But it is also 1985. But it is also 1996. But it is also 1957. For a moment, it is 1962, but then there is a slide, like tipping down a long hallway, and it is 1972. The slide shakes the ground under Arthur's feet and he falls over an open door like a gaping mouth and into 2001. He is lost. He is lost in time. It is 1966 and he is studying for the bar exam and feeling the stress like a living thing breathing down his collar. He is confused though. He looks at his hands. They are not a law student's hands. They are much older. They are wrinkled, covered in liver spots. The skin is thin and papery. Whose hands are these? What is happening? He should be at a desk in the law library at Columbia, but he sees pavement under his feet and grass growing over the shoulder of a road. Is he walking? Where is he going? There is a slide. It is 1952. He is going to meet his sister to pick apples for pie at the orchard, isn't he? But it's cold, colder than it should be for this time of year. He looks down at himself and he's in pajama bottoms and a tee-shirt, the flaps of his robe whipping in the March wind. It is raining, but his mother gave him a hat to wear, didn't she? He reaches for the top of his head and where is his hair? He cries out. He is eleven and where is his hair? He sees a yellow line in the road and aims for it, his gait growing more unsteady with every step. If he can just get to the yellow line everything will sort itself out. He just has to make it to the hospital to check on Tildie before visiting hours are over. It's only about another mile to the student union and he must have had too much to drink already because he's-

A bright light appears behind him and he hears loud honking. He lunges out of the way and a car passes down the road, horn blaring, angry shouts coming from the window as the car speeds by. Arthur is frightened. Why is he in the road? He was sitting with his grandchildren, wasn't he? The rain is coming down harder and he's cold on top of it. Where is he? How did he get here? Where was Ronan? Didn't he have a play coming up? There is a flash of blue and red lights and a siren burps at him. He is shaking, tears spilling from his cheeks into the rain. A big man is approaching him and he shrinks away, falling onto the pavement, hands up over his face to protect him from blows. The man is talking to him in soothing tones, but his roommate got beaten up bad at a peace rally and he knew better than to trust the bulls. He is crying freely now and the big man tries to get an arm under him. He skitters away, kicking at the man. The clubs will come now - it was the riots all over again. What year was this? And now he's struggling and shrieking and clawing at the man's eyes, delirious with terror. There is an ambulance now and why won't anyone tell him where he is? Why is he out in the rain in his bedclothes? This is undignified and certainly not what he expected when he set out down the road to pick apples with his sister. There is a woman. Is it Anya? *Oh Anya, you have to talk to these crazy people, I don't know what's happening.* A hypodermic appears in the woman's hand and he struggles again, but the officer holds him fast. The needle plunges into the meat of his shoulder and a warm tingling sensation floods through his system. It is 1999. And it is 1946. And it is 1982. And it is 1974. And it is 1969. But it is 2021 and the drugs caress him, softening him, unmooring him, melting him like butter, blurring his vision and slaking the last of the strength from his bones. It is 2021 and Arthur sees, in a sudden moment of terrible clarity, exactly where he is.

It is 2022 and Arthur is at the sea. The sun is shining and there is a dog running down the beach, pelting towards him as fast as he can. The dog is leaping up on him and it's Max, his old retriever from childhood. He hasn't seen Max in 70 years, but he'd know that mutt anywhere. A girl is coming down the beach. Her hair is white from the sun and he hears a familiar laughter that fills his heart with joy. It is Matilda. Matilda. Oh God, it is Matilda. And she is in his arms and they are crying and he knows it won't be long now.

It is 2022 and Arthur is going home.

Chapter Eight

Anya found him outside smoking cigarettes. He'd gone through four already and he saw no end in sight. He'd quit five or six times over the last thirty years or so. His longest stretch was over a year, but it was always stress that brought him back into the fold. Ronan supposed even if he'd quit for ten or twenty years, this singular, awful moment in time would break his streak regardless.

"Why don't they have bars in hospitals, huh?"

"Come on, Ronan."

"No, I'm serious. Everyone needs a fucking drink in a place like this. And if you have too much, hey hey, there's docs on call to pump your stomach."

"Stop bullshitting. This isn't your act."

He ignored her.

"The hospital would make some money. It would certainly make this bitter fucking pill go down easier. Hell, intensive care karaoke. I think it's fucking genius."

"Would you stop."

He took a drag and eyed his sister.

"I can't go back in there," he said.

She touched his sleeve.

"I can't."

"Take a minute. Get yourself situated and we'll go back in together. You shouldn't have been alone when-"

"Jesus, Anya, what happened to him?"

Ten years is what happened, don't act like you don't know.

She was silent for a long while, seemingly like she had the same thought he did.

"You've been gone…" she managed.

He sighed, shoulders sagging, unable to believe more shame was possible, but the well ran impossibly deep.

"He'd been going downhill. He didn't know where he was. He was getting violent with mom. We were talking about assisted living and then he got pneumonia."

"The tube."

She nodded.

"They intubated him. But this is a hospice situation now."

She squeezed him.

"They're just making him as comfortable as they can."

The shakes had subsided and the tears had run their course. Ronan felt steadier, but there was a deeper wound now, a wound of deep regret.

I wanted to talk to him. God dammit, I needed to talk to him.

"'My flesh and my heart may fail, but God is the strength of my heart and my portion forever.'"

He yanked his arm away.

"Spare me the Jesus bullshit, will you?"

"Ronan-"

"For fuck's sake, Anya. Enough with all that."

"Don't negate my faith," she warned.

"Don't presume your faith speaks for both of us," he returned.

They stood in a silent stalemate, Ronan smoking, Anya rubbing her arms against the chill. He finally relented, removed his jacket, and wrapped it around her shoulders. He put his forehead against hers, taking in her clean, familiar scent.

"Now why didn't God make you tougher in the cold?"

She butted his forehead gently with her own.

"It doesn't work like that, dummy."

"Mysterious ways?" he asked.

She nodded and took his hand like she did when they were little.

"He got you here, didn't He?"

She pulled at him, tugging him away from his smoking circle. He flicked his butt into the hedges and felt his resistance melt. As long as Anya was here, maybe he could stomach this agonizing situation a little longer. By the time they got inside, she was no longer leading him and they walked arm in arm to the elevators.

* * *

"Ronan," his mother said. "You're skin and bones!"

"Hi ma."

"Don't they feed you anything out there?"

Instantly, he was ten years old again, grinning sheepishly at his mother while she fussed over him - pants too short, cowlicks like sprung clock springs all over his head, nervous and skinny. It was easier to avoid over the phone or her godawful FaceTime calls at the crack of dawn (*Ma, it's four in the morning out here!*), but in the full face of her fawning stare, he melted. He felt, in a part of himself he hated, his posture stoop, trying to shrink himself down to her size. He felt that irresistible urge to surrender, to curl into a small ball at the foot of the bed and let her stroke his hair and coo at him and spoon feed him inane little kindnesses like a newborn.

Never a towering woman, Katherine Besso (Kathy to her friends and Kay to her husband) was a short, round fusspot who could cook a five course meal for half the neighborhood and still have the time and energy to help him with his math homework and prepare bag lunches for the troops in the morning. But in the harsh, unflattering light of the hospital Ronan could see she'd shrunk further, a silly dwarf of a woman he could probably pick up and toss over his shoulder.

He noticed something else too. She'd grown harder since the last time he'd seen her. She wore the thousand yard stare of the long time caregiver. It was the look of someone who had witnessed the slow disintegration of her lifelong partner's mind and body. It was the look of one who had fallen victim to his wild mood swings, worsening confusion, and black lapses in memory, like multiplying moth holes in an old sock. This was a feeding and changing look. Here was a woman who dealt with late nights and waking nightmares and fearfully called the police when he took off raving down the block.

Ronan had done a USO show a few years back at Camp Pendleton for Marines returning from one desert shithole or another. The USO took great care of him and the Marines were a fun and rowdy crowd. They took him to shoot off rifles at the range and he drank with them like it was his job. But he never did another show for the military, and mostly because that thousand yard stare unnerved him for weeks and months afterward.

They laughed, sure. They partied, sure. They were good kids (and kids they were, half of them easily still in their teens). But they were haunted by blood and the pop of automatic gunfire, baked by arid desert winds, and hard in a way that frightened him. They looked ancient, veterans of crimson battles who had seen and done what he never could, peering out from children's bodies with eyes like steaming red coals.

After Matilda died, Katherine had folded into worry. There was no peace and no rest. She was a worry machine, wheels spinning constantly, fretting and frowning about phantom terrors behind every door and around every corner. She called and messaged and demanded check-ins like a schoolgirl crush who stalks and suffocates their love and squeezes them until they can scarcely breathe. She paced late at night, fluffy bathrobe cinched tight at her waist, mumbling to herself, checking door locks and window latches, testing the perimeter like any good sentry must.

The night of Tildie's funeral she got drunk on cooking wine and cried and screamed and howled. Like a feral cat, she struck out at anyone who tried to comfort her and yowled herself into the tight ball of a grieving heart. The next morning, she slept in - an occurrence so rare it could be counted on one hand. She woke in misery and told the kids and her husband to fend for themselves for breakfast - an occurrence that had never happened. She drove to the cemetery and spent most of the afternoon there by herself.

Ronan didn't know what happened during those hours and it hurt him to imagine it, but when she came back, she was changed. A vigilance had emerged, poking out of her like new growth in an old garden. She dumped out all the booze in the house and carried the empties clanking out to the recycling bins in the garage. She never drank again.

The meals resumed and she busied herself with house chores like she was driven. She threw herself into the lives of her remaining children and doted over their father in a way that, if it were anyone else or observed from the outside, would seem excruciating and fake.

Worry became her drink. She took too much of it and started to need it, carved a life around it, and let it become a vital, breathing part of her anatomy. In the end, like any addiction, worry took her, eclipsed her reason and reality, and futilely served to feed the gaping maw of her loss.

Her hands had gnarled. Her hair was graying, frayed and wiry and untamed. Her back had bowed and her apple cheeks had hollowed. Her lips had thinned and her eyes were drawn. The once twinkling gaze had flattened and the crows feet had stretched and spread. The bags under her eyes were black and deep set. Even her wonderful robust plumpness had fallen to sagging and looking at her was like looking out at a sea of broken Marines who could never ever go back to who they were.

She doesn't have long either.

He brought a hand to his forehead and pressed between his eyebrows to quiet the rising chorus.

How long before you're back out here for another one, Ronan?

"My trainer has me on a super strict diet."

She shook her head, troubled as always. She looked to the ceiling, an old habit that still managed to both charm and irk him, like she was talking to God himself.

"His trainer!" she exclaimed.

"Check out my guns, ma."

He approached her, leaning in, flexing his bicep for her to squeeze. She swatted his arm away and pulled him in for a hug.

"Oh Ronan," she said, squashing herself into him. "I'm so glad you're here."

Anya glared at him and rolled her eyes while they hugged. Ronan could do no wrong in his mother's eyes. He was the favorite, firstborn and successor to the throne.

"Mama's boy."

Katherine turned on her, exasperated, and grabbed her by the sleeve of her blouse, pulling her into the hug like a whirling tornado drags a house up off its foundation. Anya tripped, caught herself, and then melted into the tangle of arms and bodies with a groan. For a moment, there was only warmth and the steady beep and hiss of machinery.

* * *

Two hours later and Ronan was climbing the walls. It was too hot in the room and he was feeling a bizarre combination of sleepiness and irritation. His mother was going on about recipes, recent obituaries, and Rotary Club drama, talking around the elephant in the room by filling the silences with nonsense. Anya, sullen and silent, held their father's hand and nodded at the right cues. She was nursing something, some secret suffering that had nothing to do with the present situation. At any other time, Ronan would dig, but he could feel his patience slipping and the chorus in his head was ramping up again.

He made a show of yawning and stretching in his seat.

"Well, sports fans," he said, his father's favorite saying. "I had a long flight in and I think I'm fading here."

"Yesterday," Anya mumbled.

"What's that?" he asked.

"You flew in yesterday, Ronan."

But Katherine was nodding.

"Jet lag, I'm sure," she said.

Anya sighed loudly.

"I made up the guest room for you."

Ronan did quick sums in his head. The kids would still be up and the little ones would climb over him like a jungle gym. And he was in no mood for his brother-in-law, conspicuously absent from this family reunion (*Is that what's up her ass, I wonder?*), and his passive aggressive barbs about Ronan's heathen and self-indulgent lifestyle. Staying with Anya was inevitable. She'd lose her mind if he snubbed her hospitality, but he thought a shoddy motel was just his speed right now, at least for the night. He got up and stretched again.

"I made a reservation at a motel for the night," he lied. "It's all good."

Anya looked at him, wounded.

"I didn't want to put you out," he said.

"God forbid."

Katherine interjected.

"I don't want you staying in some flea trap, Ronan."

He waved her off.

"I'm on the road all the time, I don't even think about it."

She made to fuss, but he was already moving. If he hashed it out with them much longer they'd wear him down and guilt him into Anya's place and-

Jesus Christ, give me a goddamned minute away from this fucking sauna.

He grabbed his jacket off the chair and bent down to kiss his mother. She smiled up at him and patted his arm. He went to kiss Anya, but she turned her head.

"I'll be at your house in the morning and we'll all go to breakfast."

She said nothing.

"Breakfast, Anya," he said. "And I'll stay. Okay?"

She gave him a terse nod and it was like the starting gun at a race. He hightailed it out of the room and moved briskly down the hall. He wasn't running this time, but he wasn't wasting any time either. When he got outside, he swallowed great gulps of cold air and felt his head clear. He was still unsteady, blindsided by the whole afternoon. He knew intellectually what he was here for and what was still to come, but the gruesome reality of it had hijacked him and was holding him hostage, demanding that he look, demanding that he sit and look it all right in the face. He wasn't ready. He would never be ready. Not for this.

But he didn't throw up this time, and that at least felt like an improvement.

Chapter Nine

Ronan was going about fifteen miles over the speed limit and had taken a sharp corner when he saw the red and blue flashes in his rearview.

Fuck! Terrific.

He slowed and pulled the Caddy over into a rut on the side of the road. Light washed over his car in steady pulses. He produced his license and rummaged around in the glove box for the temporary registration. He was sober, thankfully, but he had drugs in his bag and didn't know how a new car with temp tags and an out-of-state license was going to play out. Who knew what flavor of law enforcement he was going to get on a Saturday night. He hoped it wasn't some power tripping, don't-try-that-shit-in-MY-town type who had a hard on for out-of-towners, especially ones from Cal-i-forn-eye-aye.

The cruiser hung behind him, intimidating. He rolled down his window, papers at the ready. He felt cool and in control, surprising given his mental state since seeing his father. Time slowed and Ronan debated getting out of the car, but discretion and not a little bit of self-preservation kept him firmly in his seat. There was a squelching noise and a voice boomed behind him from a loudspeaker.

"Step out of the vehicle."

He wasn't afraid yet, but alarm bells were ringing. This wasn't standard protocol for a traffic stop, was it? The voice came again, loud, commanding.

"Step out of the vehicle now."

Ronan gulped and unclipped his belt. He lay his papers on the dash in front of the steering wheel and opened the door. He got out slowly, hands first, palms open to show nothing in his hands. He turned towards the cruiser, squinting under the harsh lights. He waved awkwardly to show he was friendly. He thought about walking toward the car when the voice came again.

"Hands on the roof of the car, legs spread."

"Officer, I think there's been a misunderstanding-"

"I said against the car."

Ronan understood his privilege. He wore it as modestly as he could, but he understood it nonetheless. Living in big cities had opened his eyes to a melting pot of races and cultures living in close proximity. But it also exposed him to a lot of ugly truths about how "the other" was treated. He wasn't black or brown. He looked the part, didn't he? He could pass, as the armchair racists liked to say. He knew how much worse this could be on its own, but he still felt a chill run through him. He hugged the door, pressed up tight against it, hands above his head, arms spread eagle. He widened his stance, lowered his head, and waited. The lights shone on, flashers lighting up the trees in the woods at the edge of the road, casting menacing shadows.

"You've lost weight," the voice over the loudspeaker said.

He turned his head toward the cruiser, trying to make sense of what was happening.

"What?"

An agonizing pause, then: "You don't call. You don't write."

That voice. He knew that voice. He heard a door open and heavy boots step out onto the pavement. He squinted in the light, trying to see something through the glare. A dark shadow materialized, moving steadily toward him. The shadow coalesced into khaki duty pants, a polo shirt and a tactical vest, a shaved head, a beard, and a mischievous grin he'd know just about anywhere.

"Ronan Besso, as I live and breathe."

Ronan broke free from the car, laughing.

"Fowler. Jesus," he said.

The man pulled him into a tight bear hug and Ronan took in the timeworn scent of coffee, cigars, and aftershave.

"I heard you were coming into town. Wanted to give you the best welcome I know how."

"You motherfucker. I almost shit my pants."

"That would make frisking you awkward."

Ronan looked at him.

"Wait? What?"

The man shook him by the shoulders.

"I'm fucking with you," he said. "But we are drinking. Right now."

"I…"

"Don't bullshit me, Ronan."

There was a long pause. This was the Hollywood way, Ronan knew it all too well. Some light chit chat, some feigned interest, creating intimacy by remembering some minute detail about the other person. Then promises to do lunch or grab a drink at some nebulous date on the calendar of someday. What came after was absence, distance, until your orbit brought the same people back around again for another meaningless greeting. Fowler knew all this. Long before the Hollywood way, he knew it as Ronan's way. Ronan never would have called him while he was in town and both of them knew it. This was how you got his attention now, via unconventional means. The two went back a long way. Didn't Fowler deserve at least a heads up he was coming from the man himself? Ronan felt even more guilt rising from a seemingly bottomless well of it deep down inside.

"I'll follow you?"

The man nodded.

"Giddy up," he said and began to walk back to his cruiser.

Ronan climbed inside his car with a mighty exhale. He put his belt back on and followed his friend onto the road. Fowler led them down familiar streets, each twist and turn rewinding Ronan in time, leading him back to a place he hadn't haunted in close to thirty years.

* * *

Fowler popped the tab off a can of beer and handed it to Ronan. He took it gratefully and drained half the can in one big swallow. He burped loudly and his friend patted him on the back.

"For the record, you were speeding."

Ronan drained the beer and threw the empty far out from his perch on top of the water tower into the woods below.

"Oh, I know."

"Are you holding?"

"Does the pope shit in the woods?"

Fowler shook his head.

"Some things never change."

Ronan held his hands out, wrists together.

"Gonna cuff me, officer?"

"That's Detective Sergeant, thank you very much."

Ronan drew back.

"Woah! Big promotion, sir. Nice work. And here I thought you were just a dumb cop."

Fowler laughed and passed him another beer.

"I am a dumb cop," he said. "Just a little smarter than the other dumb cops."

"In the valley of the blind, the one-eyed man is king?"

Fowler sipped his beer and smiled.

"Something like that."

They drank in comfortable silence for a while, looking out at the lights of the town, twinkling and stretched out before them. Nathan Fowler, Detective Sergeant Nathan Fowler, had led them out past the old granite quarry and the middle school softball field to the water tower. This was their place when they were kids. In the old days, they threw a wool fire blanket over the barbed wire fence that surrounded the tower and clambered over the side like monkeys. The long climb up the rusty ladder was a right of passage, equal parts terrifying and liberating as each rung took them farther away from the comforts below and up into something perilous and freeing.

The tower was a pale robin's egg blue, with the town's name stamped across it in big block letters. From the railing around the base, they could see the whole area - their small town nestled in the valley and the surrounding hills and forests stretching out for miles in all directions. At the very edge, the ocean, a pale green line of water that hugged the shoreline, stretching as far as the eye could see. Most of the town's water came from reservoirs now and the tower was on the docket for decommission at every town council meeting Ronan could remember. But the cost and the headache never seemed worth it and so the blue sentinel remained, standing over them like a watchtower of old.

It was cold at the top and wind chewed at them unabated. The cold felt good, it cleared Ronan's head and shook out some of the heat and claustrophobia from his body. The beer was welcome, gentler than the hard stuff, easier on his stomach, and finished with a soft mellow afterglow that softened his edges.

Fowler, once a skinny kid with wild brown hair, had thickened and solidified, broadening out into a dense barrel of muscle. He looked like a wrestler, thick in the chest and shoulders and his belly, even with the telltale protrusion of middle age, still seemed solid and strong. Baldness suited him, framing his face and highlighting his beard, lending him a lumberjack ruggedness that was a far cry from their heyday in high school. The years had been good to him and it seemed he'd found his place in the world.

Ronan was terrible at keeping in touch. He has been ghosting people before the term even became a thing. Time passed differently for him, a puzzling dilemma that made him wonder quite often if he was destined to face his father's fate of Alzheimer's one day. He'd get messages or phone calls, mean to respond, and then lose time. After a week or two or sometimes longer, he'd respond as if he had just received his messages. Most of his long time friends were used to it, but he had turned off plenty of people in his day with his loose priorities and wandering attention span.

It was never malicious, it was simply a matter of mathematics. There was only so much energy to go around, only so much in his tank on a given day. For all of Ronan's performative nature, he remained very much an introvert. Long stretches around people drained him so thoroughly he needed even longer stretches to recoup the lost wattage. Performing was exhausting. At least on stage engagement was on his terms. In real life, it felt like a constant bleeding to be on, be attentive, all the things he was expected to be, but in truth was not.

He had Facebook, but rarely updated it, Instagram, but rarely posted, and a vacant Twitter account that had all of three tweets on it and a meager collection of followers. His agent had been all over him about social presence and how ignoring it was leaving money on the table, but he couldn't be bothered. Instead, he paid two 20-something wunderkinds a fairly reasonable (in his eyes, at least) amount of money to manage his "official" accounts and post show dates and breadcrumbs for the fans.

Most of the family had regretfully come to accept his lone lighthouse keeper ways, though it still irked Anya sideways. Being on the road a lot was the best excuse he could come up with and, in many ways, legitimate enough to pass scrutiny when someone raised a stink. *It's not that I don't like people,* he'd said once in a bit, *it's that I'm continually disappointed by them.* The bit got laughs, but he had been deadly serious. He was also self-aware enough to know that anything he didn't like in someone else was a direct reflection of his own fears and insecurities. Keeping some distance was the best way he knew to prevent others from truly seeing him and coming away with their own crushing disappointment.

Half the reason he and Margot worked at all was because she fucked off and left him be most of the time. Ronan couldn't fathom marriage or children, he just couldn't get his head around it. The same person, the same life, on a repeating loop as you sag and fall apart and listen to the same stories and fight the same fights and fuck in the same boring missionary position on birthdays and holidays. It was the ultimate personification of prison and the thought of it made him feel claustrophobic and itchy in his palms. Christ, he couldn't even stand himself without frequent intoxication and gallows humor. The thought of bringing someone else into that mess and dealing with their bullshit on top of his own was grotesque.

Underneath, in the disquiet below his bristling reservations, there was a quiet voice that told him maybe he was this way because he watched his littlest sister die horribly and he just wasn't built to risk that level of loss again. The voice was softer and gentler than most of the others and easier to ignore. It may one day have its full say, they all did in the end, but for now, Ronan simply convinced himself he was better off alone.

Still, sitting in the October dusk with his old friend felt good and Ronan realized that he'd missed him. Nate had always had a sense of duty and responsibility that far eclipsed that of the other kids in their high school crew. He was the one who took car keys from drunk kids and broke up fights in the schoolyard. He'd always looked after Ronan and Ronan-

You left him behind. Didn't you, asshole? That's exactly what you did. You turned your back on him and you waltzed off into the sunset, just like you always do.

Why? Why would he do that? The question dug at him and deeper than that, far more disconcerting, was another: Why was it so easy to do? How come he didn't think about Fowler one iota the second he was out of his sightline? While Fowler kept in touch with his family, called him on his birthday, and fed him beers, somehow knowing exactly what simple comforts he still needed after all these years.

Because you're a selfish prick and that's why no one loves you.

"I'm sorry I haven't stayed in touch," he said at last.

Fowler sipped his beer and looked down over the town. The first of the streetlights started to come on one by one. He said nothing. Ronan did think he could bullshit for a moment, tell his friend about an endless parade of sterile hotel rooms and rental cars and travel reward miles. He could preen about Netflix and pornstars and whispers of a movie deal that was coming down the pipeline. He could always use his dad as an excuse, God knows he'd done it before (*Yeah sorry, my dad's been real sick, there's a lot going on right now…*), but all of that rang hollow and cheap. He knew he didn't owe an explanation to his friend and he also knew that Fowler didn't expect one, but he owed one to himself at least.

"I'm a shitty friend."

Fowler tapped his beer can against Ronan's.

"I appreciate you saying that," he said. "But you're not. You're just you. I kind of think of you like an astronaut."

Ronan laughed.

"How do you figure that?"

Fowler pointed up to the night sky and the emerging stars above them.

"They have families and people who love them, but they still leave and go up. They have to go. You get that, right? They just *have* to. The pull to be out there is so great, it will never be enough down here. Something pulls you too. It has since we were kids. I can't be pissed at you for following it."

Ronan took this in, staring down at the town below, wondering what his life would have looked like if he stayed.

"Well, I'll tell you, you're a hell of a lot more gracious about it than my family, that's for damn certain. How's yours by the way?"

Fowler drained his beer.

"Dad's finally retired - they had to drag him out and now he's loving it and wondering why he didn't do it sooner. And mom's puttering around with some kind of Mary Kay pyramid scheme."

"Really?"

"Essential oils." He grinned. "Don't get me started."

They laughed together. Ronan had seen the commercials with the blonde lady with big hair and the lemon dress on late night TV (*Who will you become when you embrace Bliss oils?*).

"And Allie? Did you finally put a ring on that, or what?"

Fowler stiffened and Ronan saw his jaw clench, tight. He closed his eyes and leaned his head back, banging it against the flaking metal skin of the water tower. After a long while he said the single worst word in the English language.

"Cancer."

Ronan felt his heart drop and an angry flurry of voices rose in his mind, screeching at him.

"No," he said. "When?"

"Last year."

Ronan turned on him.

"Jesus, Nate, why didn't you call me? I wouldn't have blown you off about this. I wouldn't have. God, I am fucking sorry."

Fowler crushed his can in his fist and tossed it over the edge with the others.

"It's okay. I wasn't alone. And I knew you were off in space. I didn't want to bother you with it."

Revelation came, cold and dismal and inky black, the way Ronan imagined space to really be. *Space isn't real life, Ronan.* He sunk down deep into a shadow of himself, agonized that he'd been so far out of touch with the Earth.

You are a shitty shitty friend. Hang your fucking head, space-man. Hang your head in shame.

"I'm so sorry," he managed. "Truly I am."

Fowler looked at him, appreciative.

"I came up here a lot after she passed. I used to think about jumping off. But it's better now. I only cry most days."

They were silent a long time.

"Do you want to talk about it?"

After a long pause, Fowler nodded.

"Actually I do."

They sat on the edge of the derelict water tower and Ronan did his best to be a friend again, to try and make up for all the lost time. He listened and held Fowler when he cried. He absorbed his grief and let him get out everything he'd been holding inside for the last year. Shitty friend or not, restless astronaut or no, Ronan was firmly returned to Earth now, and he was determined to make it count for something.

Chapter Ten

The young woman at the front desk was perky and flirtatious, quite the surprise at ten o'clock at night on the edge of town. Even in his disheveled state, she recognized Ronan immediately and insisted on everything from autographs to selfies while she checked him in. Fowler demanded to follow him to the motel (*You've been drinking, man. Take the police escort.*) and they'd pulled up lights blazing, like Ronan was an arriving dignitary on foreign shores.

Don't be a stranger.

I won't.

I mean it.

I won't.

"I watched your Netflix special like a hundred times!"

She punched buttons on her keyboard.

"You're so funny."

Ronan felt anything but funny at the moment. He felt washed up and old. He had been shocked and saddened by Fowler's loss and was growing to grudgingly accept his own. He wanted nothing more than a hot shower, sweats, maybe some porn, and a toot or two from the little baggie he had hidden in the bottom of a rolled up pair of socks.

The counter girl was low fruit off the tree and he knew an

invitation up to his room would be warmly received. But he also knew from too many encounters like these on the road that he'd wake up in the morning, hollowed out and filled with regret for using her. She'd gaze at him with that earnest look that made his insides crawl and he'd hate her for it. It wasn't her, it was never their fault. It was that she'd give him a moment of comfort and tenderness in the dark and the feeling of her pulling away would make him feel empty all over. As sweaty bellies separated and heartbeats slowed, she'd take her warmth with her and leave him bereft, come drying on his leg, a dismal wet spot on rented sheets the only remaining evidence to another battle of passion versus loneliness.

"I have to ask though," she said, lowering her voice to a whisper. "What happened with you and Anna Kendrick?"

She wasn't there when I woke up, kid. That's the long and the short of it. After a terrible night in a shithole just like this, I almost died, and when I woke up, she wasn't there. Oh sure, she was shooting a movie and under contract and overseas and she couldn't make it back, even on a red eye, and blah blah blah. But fuck man, not even a phone call, not even a card. I got a shitty bouquet from her agency of the kind of cheap-smelling flowers they leave in a green room with a bowl of peanut M&Ms for the talent. She'd moved on by then. Margot isn't too good at keeping secrets and I'd embarrassed her. I'd wounded her pride and I'm learning the hard way that the worst thing you can do to a woman is make her look foolish. But I thought we had something there for a minute. Something in those dreamy blue eyes made me think it was more than just canoodling amidst the paparazzi flashes. But that's the trick with actors, right? They're paid chameleons. No matter how much you convince yourself, you can never really be sure they aren't acting with you. I think she always knew she could do better. Isn't that what all you gossipy civilians really want to hear?

"We're still very close," he said, the universal answer that smoothed everything over and didn't invite any more questions.

Something in his tone made it clear she was wandering into unwelcome territory. She flushed and made a point of punching buttons on the terminal.

"I'm sorry," she said quickly. "I'm being nosy."

"It's okay, no harm done…Jacqueline," he said, reading off her plastic name tag.

She beamed at his use of her name, flushing more deeply. She touched his hand.

"Jackie please," she said. "Everyone calls me Jackie."

She passed two plastic cards nested in white cardboard holders across the counter to him.

"You're all set, Mr. Besso. Room 1536."

He took the cards and rapped on the counter with his knuckles.

"Ronan. Just Ronan. Mr. Besso is my father."

It was an old comeback, one of the oldest in the book, but it brought a fresh wave of grief that made him sag in his frame.

How long before you're using the past tense on that old line, Ronan, my man.

"Well Just Ronan," she said, breaking him from his reverie. "If you need anything, you call down to the front desk and I'll come running. I'm here 'till 2AM."

He grinned at her - she had some spunk and that made him feel younger for a welcome minute. He tipped her a salute.

"Thanks, Jackie."

He turned from the counter, shouldered his bag, and made for the row of elevators down the hall. By 2AM, Ronan hoped to be deep in a Xanax-induced coma and dreaming of simpler days. But the smell of her perfume followed him down the hall and he wondered.

* * *

Dear Ronan,

I want to know what it felt like. You never talk about it. You're an open diary about everything else. You leave yourself wide open, recklessly, carelessly, but somehow like you planned it too. You act like you've laid a trap. You leave yourself with your pages rustling in the wind of your laughter and you invite us to read you. Will we pick you up or will we walk on by? Will we cave to our cat-killing curiosity or will our better angels prevail? You already know the answer, don't you? You're counting on human frailty, on transgression. You're counting on us being too weak to walk away from an open book. You are far more treacherous than you ever let on, Ronan. I think I may be the only one who can see it, the blood drying on the ink of your invitation to peek.

You did that whole bit about rehab and, arguably, it was hilarious, but you kept the best parts to yourself. You always do, you selfish little piggy. Hoarding your spoils from the realm of the dead in the endlessly repeating pockets of your technicolor dreamcoat. Haven't I given to you? Didn't I roll myself in a carpet and sneak my way into your palace? Hail Caesar! Didn't I ply you with my charms and my sweet, tight heat and the outfits and scenes you love so much? Didn't I open you, Ronan? Didn't

I introduce you to pleasures you never dreamed possible in your whitebread, plain vanilla ice cream, basic bitch of a life? Don't you love the rank stench of this hot garbage poured into an hourglass dress?

Did you think that was free? Did you think I did all that out of the kindness of whatever passes for my heart these days? All relationships are transactional and you'd best figure that out before the bill comes due. Our contract is written in come and squirt with the razor-tipped pen of the dopamine hit, writ large on the canvas of all the delicious things we do when we mash our bodies together. You knew this, and you signed it just the same, didn't you, Doctor Faustus? You signed it and I want my pound of flesh from you.

So tell me what it felt like. To die. I must know. I must. Do I need to say the magic word? Do you need me to say it? To speak to you on my knees? Fine. I know what I am. Do you, I wonder? I do wonder that. Fine. It's fine. Please. Please tell me where the ferryman took you. Tell me. For fuck's sake, Ronan, tell me what you saw!

You are braver than I am. I hate that about you. I hate that I, who has gone to places most women fear to tread, still lack the singular courage to break my earthly chains. I love suicides. I love them! They are the best of us. Like explorers of old, they march to the very edge of the map (Here there be tigers!) and then over, tumbling into the unknown mystery - the only mystery that matters as far as I'm concerned. You can call it an OD. You can aw-shucks it like you always do and spin it and finesse it into a careless whoopsie. A rookie mistake. But I know. I will always know. It's intent that commits the crime, and you were fixing to check out. The killing of a man. A homicide. I see glossy crime scene photos of a naked man in a tub with a tube around his arm and a needle on the floor. His eyes are wide and staring off, looking at something with such trembling awe it makes his putrefying corpse look beautiful. This town loves you and you will fall up for the rest of your life, but you are a killer, Ronan. Willful, remorseless, colder on the inside than the naked crest of Everest, you are a smiling assassin.

I need nothing. I've been raped, beaten, burned, scarred, humiliated, left for dead and betrayed so many times I only see trust as an arcane word in an Old English dictionary now. But like the survivor I am, I proceeded to climb out, climb up, dust myself off and now I fuck the world for all to see. Because in fucking the world, I damn near guarantee to own those things they've always said about me. They are mine and mine alone. Slut. Whore. Tramp. Dirty little truck stop cocksucker. Whatever. You all watch me now. You all bow at the altar of my pinkest parts and your wives and girlfriends feel more threatened by me than the preying home invaders watching them undress through the hedgerow. I've broken up more marriages than infidelity and I want you to hate me. I want you to sulk in your shitty third floor walkup, in your leggings and your chunky sweater, on your fourth glass of chardonnay with your Live Laugh Love sign mocking you over the television and Taylor Swift propping you up so you can finally go ahead and check his browser history. Hate me to your fluttering heart's content, but you know my name, don't you? And you? You're a fucking nobody.

I need nothing. But I need this. From you. I need this from you. You alone can give it to me and that stings like a scorpion tail at high desert noon. Tell me what it felt like to die. Tell me what you saw. I won't let it happen to you again. Not before you tell me. I told you to return to me and I mean it. I will defy physics and rip the very fabric of space and time and tesseract to you. I will savage you awake. I will reach down through the cage of your ribs and grasp the red meat of your stilled heart and shock you back to life because it is my decree. If we go, we go together. I can't bear the weight of such a launch alone. Don't you hear me? I can't bear it.

Just tell me it's not void and blackness and a poured out cosmos bereft of stars. God, please tell me it's not nothing. Because at night, when everything else has had its say and I'm finally alone, it's the one thing I can't stop thinking about.

It's the only thing left in this burning world that scares me.

Lovingly,

Margot

* * *

Ronan sat on the edge of the tub in the bathroom of the hotel suite, staring at the small white rock, lovingly wrapped in cellophane. He swore to himself that he would bury his father sober. He owed Arthur at least that much. The man had suffered for years, surely his absent son could suffer through a few days and weeks of lucid, unflinching grief. But he took the coke anyway, didn't he? Sitting in the bathroom, it occurred to him that he really brought drugs for after, not during. But trying to keep or ration cocaine was a joke far funnier than anything he'd ever tell. Cocaine was ephemeral, fleeting, soaking and total like summer thunderstorms. It demanded consumption and resisting that call was a losing bet. A clean white spike that pierced straight up into the control room of the pleasure centers of the brain and jacked that reactor towards meltdown. There was no saying no to that. Even when he'd stayed away for months at a time, he'd dream about snowy lines of electric sex in his sinuses with a drip he could still taste in the back of his throat upon waking.

He knew if he unwrapped his treasure, he'd bang out some lines, put on his headphones and bounce off the walls for awhile blasting tunes. He also knew he'd call downstairs (*Well hello, Just Ronan, something I can help you with?*) and dawn would come fast and hard and punish him for trying to look head-on at the great god Bacchus. He had his sister and his brother in law and their tiresome brood in the morning and he'd have to go to the house and check on the state of affairs with his mother. He needed sleep. He truly needed sleep and there was no way he could blow Anya off again.

Fuck that. And fuck them. Your father is dying and you can do whatever you want.

But that was the white army talking. A tiny regiment of barbed ecstasy was eager to cascade through his brain, lighting up neurons as they bounced between the tender folds of his limbic system. He could flush it. He should flush it. And wouldn't that be something? Ronan Besso turns over a new leaf and leans into his second act a new man. His father would be genuinely proud of him. But he knew himself better than that. That kind of bullshit only happened in the movies and badly scripted ones at that. People changed glacially, if at all, and he knew his redemption ship had long ago sailed for fairer shores.

He looked into the tub, staring at a drip of water from the faucet. Drops fattened and glistened and then fell with an almost inaudible splash to the drain. The first and only time he'd done heroin had been in a tub exactly like this one, after the worst set of his life in a smoky Chicago speakeasy. One of the musicians helped him score and he was off to the races. He had wanted to die that night. He'd go senile into a nursing home and march to his grave before he'd ever confess that little tidbit to anyone, but he wanted out.

The goddamned management found him because he'd maxed out his credit card and still owed for another night. His heart had stopped for seven minutes on the table in the ER and he woke in an empty room with no one worrying after him at his bedside, a wound somehow worse than what put him in that tub in the first place. In the interim places, he'd seen…God what had he seen? Could he even describe it? Did he possess the vocabulary? It wasn't trumpets and angels, that was for sure. But it wasn't lights at the end of tunnels or ghosts from his past either. It was rooms upon rooms upon rooms, layering over each other in checkerboard patterns, moments of his life unfolding in each, infinite possibilities of what he'd done, what he could have done, and what he never did. He shook with the feeling that everything that was happening to him had always happened and would always happen. It was heavy fucking space science from the planet Tralfamadore was what it was. It was like the end of that Christopher Nolan movie with the black hole in it.

"It's not nothing, Margot," he said. "I don't know what it is, only that it's way bigger than we can comprehend. But it's not nothing, I can promise you that."

He was starting to feel depressed and debated calling her. A little dirty talk and some phone sex and then the kind of sleep that only comes after a good orgasm would do him right. But his hands, traitors that they were, found themselves unpacking the little bundle. The first of that baking soda, detergent smell wafted into his nostrils and the hairs on his forearms stood up. He fished a razor blade and a travel mirror from his toiletry bag and set to work.

He stared down at the parade of carefully cut lines on the mirror and felt all the guilt and shame and exhaustion he'd been harboring pushed aside by the simpler machinery of greed. He dove in and the machinery took over, riding him well into the morning.

Chapter Eleven

Ronan hovered at the doorbell and steeled himself for the onslaught. The morning had been shaky and too bright and he managed to punch himself awake only with the help of bitter black motel coffee and one last snort from his stash. Wayfarers hid the worst of it, but he looked spectral in the sunlight and he couldn't help flinching at loud noises. He was smart enough to stop at a florist and spend an amount that felt like extortion (flowers and cakes were the biggest rackets on planet Earth, as far as Ronan was concerned) on a bouquet of seasonal whatever for his sister. Pretty things spackled over a lot of kicked-out holes in the walls between them and somewhere in the meticulously kept ledger she kept of his successes and failures, he'd win points for the thought.

The kids would get spoiled rotten for the rest of the time he was there, so he didn't worry about showing up to them empty handed. His brother-in-law could have nothing and like it. Ronan had his problems with Anya, there was no getting around that, friction was half the glue that held their relationship together, but Ted was a whole other story. The only thing worse than an unemployed musician was an unemployed musician who knocked up his sister, not once but three times. There were rumors they were trying for a fourth.

Jobs shackled Ted, they ground down his free spirit and assaulted his delicate sensitivities. He resented that a Berklee dropout could be forced to don the yoke of the everyman and surrender his big dreams for a bleak corporate hellscape. He eschewed offers of good, solid, decently paying jobs from his family and friends in pursuit of musical nirvana. He was working on a symphony. Then he was writing a Broadway show. Then he was composing sweeping scores for action hero movies. Then he was getting into ringtones.

It was always something, some harebrained scheme that was conceptually exhausting and never executed to completion. All hat and no cattle, as his father would say. Ronan and Arthur also had their problems, but they were in lockstep over their mutual derision for Ted.

Out of some cockamamie sense of Christian charity no doubt, Anya started fucking Ted, first propping up his endless plans for greatness, then supporting him financially, and finally bearing his children. Ted ultimately decided to headline a 70s tribute band, *Ted Zeppelin*, and this sad collection of balding rockers played in equally sad dune clubs up and down the coast for trashy tourists from New York and New Jersey. This strictly summer gig brought in meager earnings and winters were spent locked in fights with Anya, endless rehearsals, and hazy days of bong rips that all blended together into a cloud of general disappointment.

With each child, the burden Anya carried grew heavier and she grew harsher, more impatient, and tyrannical when it came to her family. She would make the fiercest tiger mom run screaming and dominated the homestead with an iron fist. When she cracked the whip, everyone in the house jumped.

Except for Ted. Perfectly unflappable Ted who just knew that stardom was around the corner. It made Ronan seethe. He could sympathize though, couldn't he? A struggling, starving artist himself for the better part of thirty years, couldn't he at least give Ted a little grace? Really, what was the difference between himself and Ted?

"I have fucking talent," he sneered and pushed the doorbell.

Ronan worked his ass off, hustling for his place in the sun in a tireless, unforgiving grind that threatened to break him at every turn. Not to mention Ronan was single. The thing that really got under his skin was that he knew, as much as he'd hate it and as much as he'd probably end up resenting both his wife and his kids, that he'd become a goddamned CPA before he'd let his wife shoulder the sole responsibility as breadwinner for his family.

Ted was a bum, simple as that, and Ronan prayed (Anya would be proud) with every phone call when she'd drone on about what Ted had done *now*, that she'd finally gather the courage to cut the dead weight that was Theodore Schachner and free herself.

He heard running footsteps coming down the stairs and gripped the bouquet of flowers, holding them out in front of him like an exorcist. He forced his best smile and the door opened.

✳ ✳ ✳

"Is that your car outside, Uncle Ronan?"

Benjamin-

(*About Benjamin he said: "Let the beloved of the LORD rest*

*secure in him, for he shields him all day long, and the one the
LORD loves rests between his shoulders."*)

-his youngest nephew, leaned over the back of the chair in
the dining room, swinging eight year old legs restlessly and
pointed out the window to the driveway.

"You like it, Benji?"

"It's a Cadillac! So cool!"

Anya was arranging the flowers he brought in a heavy
glass vase at the kitchen island while Ted leaned against the
counter and silently gave Ronan the stink eye.

"You rented a Cadillac?" she asked.

Ronan squirmed, seeing the future clearly, and the silence
stretched.

"Actually," he paused. "I bought it."

Anya dropped the flowers and looked up sharply.

"You *bought* a Cadillac!"

He nodded.

"So cool!"

Ruth-

(*Ruth said, "Do not urge me to leave you or turn back from
following you; for where you go, I will go, and where you lodge,
I will lodge. Your people shall be my people, and your God, my
God."*)

-the middle child, thirteen, who greeted him with a single
indifferent grunt when he arrived, her face buried in a Donna
Tartt novel, finally emerged from her book.

"How much did that set you back?" she asked, pinning
him with a shrewd glance over the rims of her glasses and
suddenly Ronan was looking at his father.

Ronan thumbed at her, grinning at Anya.

"When did Ruth turn into Dad?"

Anya stared at her daughter and rolled her eyes.

"This is a new thing."

Ronan turned to his niece.

"It didn't *set me back* too badly, thank you, Arthur," he said to her.

"So I guess you're like loaded then, huh?"

Ronan glanced at Anya again, but she just shook her head.

"Must be nice," Ruth said and returned to her book, dismissing all of them.

Ted was smiling to himself, tugging at his chin, staring down at the kitchen tile. The smile was more of a grimace and Ronan could sense him gearing up for something passive aggressive.

"Something funny, Ted?"

Ted met his gaze.

"No," he said. "I just can't imagine anyone in this family being so self indulgent."

Ronan didn't do passive aggressive. He was an in-your-face, what-did-you-just-say-to-me, kind of person and he'd stood up to tougher, meaner, and far more hostile opponents than Ted. If you counted hecklers, he was a modern day gladiator. He felt his fists clench at his sides and he wondered, not for the first time, what would happen to that blasé sanctimonious attitude if Ronan popped him a good one in the mouth. Of all the voices in his head, he heard Margot calling on him to stand down.

Be cool, baby. He's a fucking nobody. And he knows it.

"Where's Joel?" he asked, changing the subject.

A hush fell over the room and Ronan glanced around. Ted

went back to staring at the floor. Benji hung his head on the back of the chair. If it were possible, Ruth sunk even deeper into her book. Anya started stuffing flowers into the vase like they had suddenly offended her in some way.

"He's staying at a friend's," she said.

A lie. A painfully obvious lie. She wasn't even trying, and Anya could lie with the best of them. No one in the room made any attempt to refute her.

"Okay," he said. "Everything all right?"

Again, the hush. Ronan accepted he'd been away too long and that life had moved on without him. He also accepted families had secrets and private matters and he was probably the last person to dig for dirt and gossip. Rough scrapes with the paparazzi and the tabloids and the whole shitshow with Anna Kendrick had given him a newfound respect for privacy. But this was different. He expected Anya to keep things from him, that was a given, and Ted wouldn't confide in him if he was the last person on Earth. But here was a whole family in a confederacy of silence that only served to tell him, almost as if they were shouting, that something was very very wrong. He stared daggers at Anya, but she redoubled her focus on the flowers and tuned him out.

Fine. You want to play that game? I'll squeeze it out of your children.

"Who wants to go for a ride?"

He jangled his keys. Benji leapt from his perch on the chair and Ruth finally put down her book.

"Can we go to IHOP?" she asked him.

"Does the pope shit in the woods?"

"Ronan!" Anya snapped.

Ruth smirked at him.

"Rooty tooty fresh and fruity!" Benji shouted and then he was running to get his coat.

Ted left the room without another word and Anya sighed, defeated.

"Wear a coat, Ruth, it's cold."

Ruth ignored her and stood by Ronan's side at the ready. Benji returned in his coat and hat. Anya pointed pruning scissors at the assembled troupe.

"Seatbelts, all of you," she warned. "Don't drive like a maniac, Ronan."

The three saluted in unison. It tickled Ronan (*Wow, maybe I do rub off on these kids, after all*) because it was perfectly unscripted and couldn't have been choreographed any better. But Anya was tight lipped and stern, unmoved by their frivolity.

"I'll be safe," he reassured her.

He would be, but he was also going to ply her kids with sugar and foul language and larger-than-life stories until they spilled the beans. Something had tripped his defenses and it kept gnawing at him. One way or the other he was going to get to the bottom of what everyone was keeping from him.

* * *

They were on a long stretch of straight road that ran along the coastline. Beach houses on stilts dotted the periphery and in the distance was the strip of hotels and clubs that Ted would no doubt play when *Ted Zeppelin* got rolling again. Near to Halloween, the road was devoid of traffic and a steady wind ruffled the tall reeds in the dunes. Ruth gripped the steering wheel, knuckles white, eyes locked straight ahead, face set into a look of intense determination.

"Okay," Ronan directed her. "Now push down on the gas, real easy."

The Caddy lurched forward. Ruth hit the brake hard in response and they jerked to a stop.

"You're messing it up!" Benji shouted from the back seat.

Ronan put a reassuring hand on her shoulder.

"You're doing great, Ruthie, let's try it again."

She frowned and tried again. The car launched, much smoother than her first attempt and soon they were gliding along the shoulder of the road.

"Good. Now let's pull onto the road, yeah?"

She nodded, eyes never leaving the stretch in front of them. She jacked up the brake again and they pitched forward.

"It's okay, you're okay. Just remember everything's easier when you're always moving. You can just take your foot off the gas and coast. We only want to hit the brake when we need it."

She nodded again, pressing down on the gas pedal. The car zoomed forward again. He put a hand on her knee.

"Don't brake, just ease off the gas."

She followed his instruction and they felt the car slow.

"Perfect! You're getting it. Now let's pull in."

Ruth guided the car gently off the shoulder and the ride smoothed out as they connected with the asphalt. She accelerated slightly and straightened them out between the lines. She brought the car up to a respectable 30 miles an hour and they were cruising.

"Ruth?"

"Yeah?"

"You're officially driving."

She smiled. It was the slightest hitch in her lips, but Ronan could see she was pleased with herself. More so, he could see she was pleased that she was conquering something difficult. Ronan stared at her, in her wool Carhart beanie, dyed jet black hair poking out from underneath, with too much eye makeup and a slew of jewelry and bangles. She had temporary tattoos running down the length of her bare arms, prickled with gooseflesh despite the warmth from the heater. Her brown cords were threadbare, ripped at the knees, and her fingernails were a deep crimson that was almost black, even in the sunlight.

She and Benji, the whole family, had a Czech robustness they'd inherited from Ted and they all had Anya's nose and eyes. But as they grew, they each began to look more and more like Ronan's father and adopted more and more of his mannerisms, seemingly without even knowing it. He wondered if Margot was like this as a teenager, frightfully intelligent, nose in a book, rebelling against her form and station with punk rock rage. He smiled at this.

Thinking about her when she's gone now, are we? Ronan, my man, you've got it bad, don't you?

Ruth leaned her head his way, eyes still focused on the road.

"I've got buildings coming up, Uncle Ronan. What do I do?"

"Don't hit 'em!" Benji shouted, the definitive backseat driver.

"You're fine, just ease off the gas a bit and watch out for people. And yeah, like the kid said, don't hit them or you owe me sixty grand."

She clenched her jaw.

"I really wish you hadn't just told me that."

"You're fine, Ruth. Just keep on keeping on."

"Sixty grand!" Benji exclaimed, impressed. "That's like more than our house."

"No it isn't, dipshit," she said, glaring at him through the rearview.

"Eyes on the road, cadet. Dipshit will still be there when we're done."

Benji punched his arm and Ronan reached back and grabbed for his feet. They wrestled around for a bit until Ruth shouted at them.

"Hello! I'm trying to drive here, thank you very much!"

He raised an eyebrow at his nephew and they fell silent. It was one of Anya's expressions and now Ronan was looking at a smaller version of his sister and it was all too much. Genetics was one hell of a spooky discipline.

"Joel's going to be so jealous," Benji said.

Ruth chanced another baleful look at him through the rearview. Realizing his error, Benji looked down at his shoes and silently cursed himself.

"Okay Ruth, let's get to end of the road and I'll have you pull over. I think that's enough for today."

Her shoulders slumped in her seat.

"Did I do something wrong?"

"No, no way. You did great. You're already a way better driver than your dad."

The kids eased up a bit at this; Ted was a menace behind the wheel.

"But I think it's time we talk. Yeah?"

They said nothing, but he knew he'd won this fight at least.

Trap them in the car. It was his mother's oldest and favorite trick. Talk about bullshit for a bit and then lay into the heavy questions when the only way out was to dive out of a speeding car and take your chances against gravity and blacktop.

Ruth passed the strip and eased the car back over into the sandy shoulder. She started talking, haltingly and uncertain at first, but then it came rushing out of her like she'd been holding it in a long time. Benji filled in the blanks and, after a time, both of them were crying. Ronan listened, silent, studying them, never interrupting and only using his hands to goad them further into full disclosure. He listened with a seriousness he'd never possessed before and when they were finished, he left them in the car and smoked three cigarettes back to back. When he came back, Ruth surrendered the driver's seat.

"Are we in trouble?" Benji asked.

He reached out to touch both of them.

"No, you are most assuredly not in trouble," he said and pulled the car back onto the street.

But your parents are going to get read the motherfucking riot act, that I can promise you.

With all the self-control he could muster, Ronan managed the speed limit back to the house and readied himself for war.

Chapter Twelve

"When were you going to tell me?"

Anya stared at her hands.

"*Were* you going to tell me?"

She picked at her thumbnail.

"There's so much going on with Dad right now, I just didn't think-"

"Jesus fucking Christ, Anya!"

"Language," Ted said.

Ronan sneered at him.

"Fuck yourself, Ted."

Ted gestured to Benji and Ruth.

"There are children in room, Ronan. Show some respect."

Anya clapped her hands together loudly.

"And there shouldn't be. Kids, go upstairs right now, the grownups need to talk."

The two didn't budge. Ruth crossed her arms over her chest defiantly.

"Anything you have to say about Joel, you can say in front of us," she said.

Anya pleaded at her with her eyes.

"Ruth, Benji is too little for this. Can you please take him upstairs?"

"Aw, what did I do?" Benji asked.

Ruth was implacable.

"We have a right to hear."

"Ruthie, *please.*"

Ted glanced at Ronan, who tipped his head toward his sister.

"Listen to your mother, kids," Ted said at last.

"This is bullshit," Ruth said and stormed out of the room.

"Bullshit!" Benji echoed and followed her, puffing his chest and goose-stepping in line behind her.

When they were gone, Ronan rose from his chair and started poking around in the kitchen cabinets.

"Above the stove," Anya said.

He reached up and opened the doors onto an array of bottles. He took a bottle of Makers Mark from its perch.

"Cabinet next to the fridge."

He retrieved a rocks glass and paused.

"Anyone else?"

They shook their heads. He returned to the table, pouring a generous portion of the bourbon into his glass and drinking deeply.

"Like that's going to help," Ted said resentfully.

"It's going to help *me*, Theodore. Okay?"

"God knows you're so good at helping yourself."

Ronan ignored him. He reached across the table for Anya's hand. She grasped his tightly and closed her eyes, tears spilling from her cheeks.

"Sister," he said. "Please tell me what I can do."

"Oh Ronan. I don't know that there's anything you *can* do. He's…he's sick."

"I don't believe that."

"He is," she insisted.

"Troubled, sure. But tell me what seventeen year old kid isn't these days."

"Ronan…I-"

"Let me help, Anya. I want to help."

"We don't want your help," Ted cut in.

Ronan drained the rest of his glass in one gulp and slammed it down on the table.

"You have no problem cashing the checks I send each month though, do you?"

Ted rose from the table, red-faced and furious.

"How much money have you taken from Arthur?"

"I don't need to listen to this."

"You think I don't know you're just sitting around waiting to pick at his estate like a fucking vulture when he finally goes? What do you think, I'm fucking stupid?"

"I'm not going to take this from some childless man boy in my own home."

Ronan snorted.

"Your home? *Your* home? That's rich, Ted, even for you. Last I checked Anya's still the only one who pays the fucking mortgage around here."

"I'm going upstairs, I've had enough of this."

Ronan refilled his glass and raised it to him.

"Bye Theodore. See you in court, you fucking freeloader."

Ted halted at the threshold, shoulders tense.

"Do it," Ronan taunted. "Please God, do it."

The moment lengthened and Ronan could feel the first acid drippings of a wholly new sensation coursing through his veins. Bloodlust. It was bloodlust. He wanted to rip and tear and to hit something until it stopped moving. He could feel his lips separate and his canines protrude. The adrenaline, a live wire, tasted metallic and bitter and glorious. His tongue thickened and his vision narrowed to a lethal cone of opportunity. He could hear savage feminine laughter shaking through his mind.

Jesus, Margot. What are you doing to me?

Her voice, triumphant, drowning out the others, ringing through his ears, a proud Valkyrie surveying the killing fields with a blood-stained sword and wings dipped in ichor.

I am making you king, my darling.

"Enough!" Anya shouted.

She snapped them out of their standoff. Ted moved on into the other room and Ronan felt himself relax a bit. He realized he'd been gripping his sister's hand tight enough to leave marks and he released her, forcing himself to breathe deeply. He finished the last of his bourbon, feeling himself steady. The red mist receded from his vision. He rose.

"I need a cigarette."

"I'll come with," she said.

He strode out towards the back yard, hands shaking, the last dregs of adrenaline working their way through him. Ronan was angry and he was upset, and under it he was worried in way he never thought he could be, even about his own father. But he had to admit, if only to Margot, that he felt more alive than he'd felt in almost thirty years.

* * *

"Can I see him?"

She pulled her coat tighter around her.

"I don't know, he's on a hold…"

"I'm really not asking here, Anya."

"Ted won't like it."

Ronan breathed out smoke and flicked ash from the head of his butt.

"Ted can get fucked."

"Jesus, Ronan."

"What are you still doing with that dead weight? Seriously."

She watched him smoke, trying to think of an answer that would satisfy him, knowing deep down that no answer could.

"It's different when you have kids together."

"You could do so much better."

She laughed.

"I know."

Ronan stepped back in surprise.

"Wow."

"I know," she repeated. "But it's different when you have kids together. It just is."

"Is Joel okay? Medically, I mean?"

Anya ran a hand down her face.

"They stabilized him," she said. "They gave him a charcoal treatment for the drugs and he's been sober for about a week."

She choked down a sob.

"He has ligature marks around his neck. From the rope…"

She faltered then, tumbling forward. Her head shook and the tears came.

"My baby."

Ronan came to her, caught her in mid-fall, wrapping his arms around her, holding her while she heaved and wept into his shoulder.

"Ronan, my baby has rope marks around his neck."

"Okay," he said, holding her tight. "It's okay."

The rest was lost in sobs. She lost herself in his arms, hugging him fiercely, withering sobs pouring forth into the night. It was an ugly cry, devoid of restraint, devoid of the careful, conscious way Anya always held herself, even in the face of the most dismal of circumstances. It was snotty and ungracious and loud and Ronan held her, immune to the cold, untouched by the chill wind blowing down the corridors of their quaint little neighborhood.

You are king now, Ronan, Margot said to him. *Own it. Protect them now, as you would the throne. That is your job now, child king. That is your only job.*

He held her and let her cry and for a long while, her sobs were the only sound on the empty street. A full orange moon was the sole witness to a tragedy that has played for countless aeons, over and over, upon the trembling surface of the Earth.

* * *

Ronan, more than a little drunk, climbed into the big bed in the guest room with a grateful sigh. The sheets were silky and soft and fresh and the pillows collapsed under him with a gentle sigh when he lay his head down. It was his first night alone since he'd arrived and he sprawled, stretching his arms out wide and wriggling his back deeper into the mattress. He exhaled, a deep breath, driven by exhaustion. He closed his eyes and relished the all-encompassing quiet that spread across the house, the stretching, pregnant silence that only comes to a house after 2AM.

He'd brought a book and his tape recorder. He loved the old Panasonic and he carried it everywhere, filling tapes with observations, thoughts, jokes, and drunk or stoned ramblings. Tapes were getting harder to come by these days and his agent couldn't understand why he just didn't use his phone like every other person on the planet, but he refused to relinquish it. He kept his tape collection in plastic sleeves, dated and filed like library books in a curio cabinet in his bedroom. It was one of the only things Ronan was genuinely fastidious over.

He'd planned to read a bit or tape a few things, God knew there was a lot to unpack from this trip already. But the bed sung him lullabies of flannel and down and a pillow top mattress and he felt himself drifting into the arms of sleep in a place where he knew, despite all the insults tomorrow would bring, he was completely safe.

He heard the door open from very far away and then there was a gentle tugging at the sleeve of this tee-shirt, calling him back from blissful shores.

He opened his eyes to find Benji looking up at him. Ronan sat up in bed.

"Hey bud. What's up? Can't sleep?"

Benji shook his head.

"Can I sleep with you?"

Oh you are killing me, little dude.

He pulled the big comforter open and scooched over to the other side of the bed.

"Hop up."

Benji climbed into bed and curled up with him. Ronan expected to feel annoyed at the intrusion, but instead he found an odd comfort. There was something soothing about the gentle rise and fall of Benji's breathing. The child was hot and had a wild boy smell about him. Ronan closed his eyes and felt his own breathing start to match his nephew's. As he hung on the edge of sleep, he heard the door again. He opened one eye and Ruth was looking down at them.

"Room at the inn?"

Ronan nodded and she got into bed next to her brother.

"Get the light, will you," he said.

Then he was asleep.

Chapter Thirteen

He was up and out the door early in the morning before anyone woke up, leaving the kids dozing in his bed. He ate a bagel and hot black coffee at Dunkin' Donuts and scrolled through headlines absently on his phone. He passed anonymously at the dawn hour and remained in the restaurant unmolested. He wanted to get to the hospital without having to play the back and forth with the rest of them. Time felt like it was slipping faster and faster away from him and there were things he still needed to say to his father. He didn't even know what to say exactly, but he knew he had to say something. It wouldn't be regret or bitterness if he didn't get the chance, it would be incompletion, and that somehow seemed worse. Beyond closure, beyond making peace, he needed to unburden himself while there was still something left of Arthur to receive it.

He drove to the hospital and stood outside his car, smoking, stalling. He got a drag or two and then stamped the cigarette out in disgust. There was something about the early morning, whether it was sobriety, the first break of new light, or the frosty cleanness of the air, that made him aware what a smelly rotten habit he carried around with him. He breathed into his hands to warm them and made for the entrance.

Inside he smelled coffee and cooking breakfast and sickness. There was a calm to the hospital in the daybreak, a slower pace that made him feel more at ease than his last visit. He took his time, pausing at the gift shop to flip through magazines and squeeze plush animals. He opted for the stairs over the elevator and marched up six flights, forcing his thighs to flush some blood through his veins. He felt warm and awake at the top of the landing. He pushed open the fire door and walked down the empty corridor.

He pushed the door open and entered. The room lay mostly in shadow, yellow rays just beginning to slide across the walls. Machines beeped and the ventilator rose and fell with a rubber wheeze. Arthur slept under a pile of blankets, IV lines protruding out from under them, leading up to drip bags that kept him hydrated and sedated. His hair and eyebrows were wild and his beard, on a face clean shaven almost every day, was strange on his face. The wrinkles at his eyes and cheeks and forehead were canyons, deeply etched valleys, devoid of rain so long they were cracked and parched. His mouth was open in a seemingly frightened O, lips chapped and split, with the intubation tube running deep down his throat, his only link to life now. The simple task of breathing was no longer his to command.

"Hi Dad," he said and squeezed his father's foot under the blanket.

He sat down in the chair beside the bed and raised his thumb to his mouth, chewing at the nail there and watching his father. He sat this way for the better part of an hour, listening to the chirping of morning birds outside the window and the steady inflation and deflation of the ventilator. He thought he might sit like this all day, but something - not a voice from his chorus or from any conscious part of him, but from someplace wholly other - finally called on him to speak.

* * *

I got a 175 on my LSATS, Dad. I never told you. I sat for them about eleven years ago now. I took one of those prep courses on the sly on my days off. I did a bunch of practice tests but I wasn't expecting much when I took it. I don't know why I did it. Maybe to make you proud of me. Maybe to prove to myself that I really had what it takes. Hell, maybe it's because I was beaten down putting on a show every night and serving food to assholes for peanuts and fed up and willing, finally, to listen to you.

I never expected to ace them. I could have picked my ticket then. Columbia. Penn State. Stetson. Maybe even Yale or Harvard if I really tightened up my game. I started getting brochures from schools all over, even Europe. Scholarship offers, you name it. I would have been miserable. You must know that. I would have dove in, excited by the idea of starting something big. You know me, I dive in with both feet. I'm a fucking wizard at beginnings. But then I'd start to get it. It. The feeling. The fear. Trapped. Tedious. Boring. Repetitive. Labeled and predetermined. No creativity. No innovation. I'd start to feel like I was losing myself, losing who I was, following a path for the sake of safety and notoriety and making it so I could sit in a room with Anya and not feel like a failure for once. So you could look at me and finally see me as more than just a disappointment.

I never did anything with them. I put those scores in a locked drawer and started throwing out all the brochures. I had beaten it, you know? I had done a hard thing and beaten it and that was all I needed from the entire affair. I just needed to know I'd won. LSATs? The formidable front door you need to get through before you can even think about all the Clarence Darrow, Atticus Finch stuff. Buckle down. Work your ass off. These exams can make or break you. They're the difference between a being a rising star at a big wig firm or chasing ambulances from a fluorescent-lit, sticky linoleum, grease trap in a strip mall next to a liquor store. And I aced those motherfuckers without even trying.

I want you to get that. Like really get that. I didn't even try, Dad. I'm smarter than anyone in this family gives me credit for, and I got that from you. All that is good in you is also in me. I am your son, in every way but the way that matters most to you. I know you love me, I know you love us. Despite all our fights, even the mean ones, I never once felt the coldness of you pulling away from me. But I wanted your respect too. Even more than your love, I think, if I'm being honest. Your admiration. Your pride. For you to say to all your friends, that's my son! Look there, that's my son. Not when people asked you, What's Ronan doing these days? *And you'd sigh and say,* You know how kids are *or* Trying to find himself again. *I didn't want you to make excuses for me. I didn't want to have to be something you forced. Something you actively had to make palatable to save face. I wanted you to believe in me, Dad. To believe and trust that I could do it, that I had what it took to be a success in my own way. On my own terms.*

I could have been a lawyer. I could have been a good one. Or a doctor or a stock broker or any of those proud old boy roles that empires are made of. I could have been a big deal project manager like Anya or even started my own company and rolled my sleeves up and rocked my own capitalist manifest destiny. But I didn't. Not because I couldn't. Not because I'm lazy or misguided or a dreamer or rootless. But because I'm different. Do you get that? Can you see who I am, dad? Did you ever try? I am different.

For a long time, I thought that was a bad thing. I looked right and left and all my friends were getting married and buying houses and taking trips and starting families and I was still getting drunk at bars after work like an asshole. Everyone else was growing up and moving on and I was still the same Peter Pan, unchanged by time, dreaming of Wendy Darling waiting for me at her window between adventures, shocked beyond repair when I see she has grown so old in my absence. I couldn't make it work. I tried, but I couldn't make it work. I couldn't because it isn't who I am. It's not who I am. I'm built of different stuff than the rest of this family. I want different things and I approach all of this, my life, my career, my time here, from a lens that you just can't look through. I wish you could see who I am. I wish I could show you. I wish you'd given me a chance to show you.

I've been so awkward for so long now. You don't see that either. No one does. My anxiety. My raging anxiety. It's constant, ever-present. It never leaves me alone. Sometimes I feel like the walls are closing in and that every single person I see hates me. I can hear the whispers of them talking about me behind my back or feel that queer silence that settles in when you walk into a room full of people who've just been talking shit about you. I catch the briefest micro-expressions of annoyance or fatigue when I run into people in public or catch them off guard. Through some psychic sixth sense, I can feel them each withdraw, pulling away to protect themselves before my gravity traps them, the same way it's trapped all of you.

I know every phone call with me is a chore for you. I know you tolerate me, at best, and that this entire familial facade is based solely on obligation. No one fought to keep me here and I know that everyone, from Anya on down, breathed a sigh of relief when I packed up my car and rolled out. He's someone else's problem now. Let another coast deal with his moods, his abuses, his bullshit. We don't want him here. We can't take care of him anymore. We can't afford to keep bailing him out of trouble and it's growing tiresome to laugh off his career decisions at the yacht club on Thursday nights. You exhaust us, Ronan, and no one has the time or the energy to indulge your increasingly tiresome weakness.

Sometimes I close my blinds and I hide in a corner in a dark room and I rock myself back and forth because I'm so scared and I don't know why. I cringe at loud stuff and I can't look people in the eye and I stutter when people talk to me. And I sweat! Jesus, it's a fucking shitshow being in my head.

It finally came to head a few years ago. I had my first full-on panic attack before a show in Memphis. I actually thought I was having a heart attack. The room shook and my heart was beating so fast. Too fast. I was sweating and shaking and I couldn't breathe. I had spots in my vision and I was frightened of violence - like physical, take-you-out-back, take-a-lead-pipe-to-your-teeth, violence. I would have screamed if I could. Have you ever been that scared, Dad? I wouldn't wish that on anybody.

The only way I can describe it is that it was like - after all these years of suppressing it and hiding it or denying it outright - my fakeness was finally rising up in revolt. I realized how much I suck, Dad. How much I've been, and continue to be, a terrible, fucked up, selfish cock of a person. How much I've lied. How much I've bullshit people. How I use people for what I want and then move on. How I can turn on the charm and flash the smile and take from people without them ever seeing my hand in the cookie jar. How I abandon people at the first sign of trouble and how I run from hardship and responsibility like a yellow-bellied coward. How badly I treat my body, how badly I treat other's bodies. How all this, all of this, has finally caught up with me and I have nothing. I am nothing.

Then it was a candy-colored assortment of pills. The ultimate Hollywood cliche, I grant you, but there it is. Pills keep the red carpet rolled out. It's what you do now, isn't it? You have a nervous breakdown and you see a shrink and they dope you out so you can function. No one gives a rat's ass about cognitive behavior training or Jungian shadow integration or any kind of responsible therapy anymore. These shrinks are just glorified vending machines now. Pull the lever and out comes the weekly regimen. No one cares about actually helping you, it's just about giving you enough candy so you can still work and pay your taxes and hopefully not rob a bank or shoot up a movie theater.

The pills work, I have to admit that to you. But you pay a price that destroys you by inches if you let it. I feel nothing on them. Nothing, Dad. I don't get elated, I don't get furious. I don't cry, I don't panic, I don't lose my shit in traffic. I am on an even keel. Steady Eddie. Your designated driver for the evening. Real genuine human emotion has to be big to even get past the firewall, and even then, it takes a minute. There's a delay, like a long fuse on a stick of dynamite. It takes my body a minute to register what's happening and sort it into its appropriate slot. Even then it's washed out, bleached, sanitized. My world is diffused, like drops of ink in a glass of water. At first there are distinct parts of me, but they disintegrate in the water, and I spread out, losing more of myself in the water each time I take two with food and avoid drugs or alcohol.

I can function. I am a good little drone. No panic attacks. No crippling anxiety. No social paralysis. And sleep? Jesus fucking Christ, I sleep like a newborn cradled in his momma's arms. I haven't slept like this in decades. But sex doesn't interest me and I can't come and then after a while, I can't even get it up anymore and I'm okay with that. Food loses its taste. Television, concerts, clubs, all the bread and circus we count on the entertain the masses, loses its appeal. I am flat now. I am beige. I go with everything in the room, there's no clashes. Who doesn't love beige? But I can no longer stand out and I no longer care that I can't. It's a weird state, Dad. It's just fucking weird. Everything is just okay. Everything is just there. But underneath, there's this little scream all the time. It's your soul in there. Buried under the bedrock of re-uptake inhibitors, suffocating in forced pools of stagnant serotonin, your soul is screaming. I'm told if you up your dosage at that point, eventually the screaming stops.

In the midst of this, your son goes viral. Can you believe that? At a hole in Cincinnati of all places, during one of the worst sets of my life, I change course mid-way through and suddenly they're all dying on the floor and some flannel kid and his coke-skinny girlfriend film the whole thing and put in on YouTube. Suddenly, I've got people calling me and agents bidding for me and now there's contracts and lawyers and checks for sums that feel about as real as Monopoly money. Then I'm on Fallon, then I'm on Kimmel, then it's Netflix calling.

I'm going to confess to you that being on those pills is probably the only thing that got me through that first launch. You want me doing sixteen shows a week? I can do that. You want me in twenty-two states in a month for a tour? I can do that too. You want me to crap out an hour for Netflix? Check. Smile for this one. Interview for that one. Go make this hospital full of kids with leukemia laugh? Got it. Go make this platoon of sharp-eyed killers back from Afghanistan laugh? Roger that. No panic. No stress. The only way to navigate any part of this circus is to truly and wholeheartedly not give a fuck about any of it.

So what happened? I was introduced to a pretty young actress at a party in the hills. She had a killer laugh, a sick sense of humor, and the faintest edges of I-still-don't-quite-believe-I'm-here awkwardness that complements my own edges perfectly. We're cute on paper and everyone loves us and she finally makes me feel like I'm no longer trying to navigate this strange new town and this inexplicable new station on my own.

But I can't trust it. I don't trust it. I'm not feeling anything. I just put a huge tourniquet on to stop the bleeding, but I haven't dealt with anything. The bottom fell out and I realized what a fuck-up I was and how badly I hated myself. I was still there in my mind. The pills just made it okay to put all that on the backburner while life happened around me. But it's like I was being rewarded for being a fuck-up. Does that make sense? Instead of dealing or reconciling or even trying to integrate, I blew up and suddenly I've got cash and pull and an actress on my arm and I'm signing autographs in Burbank and seeing my name on theater marquees and it all feels like a dream. Like something happening to me and not because of me.

So I start doing major drugs to feel something. To start to move that iceberg that's blocking my real, unfiltered emotional self that's stifled under all this numb cold. I take it too far and three days after getting out of rehab, I meet a pornstar at a loft party downtown and she's so razor sharp, she cuts through that numb shell like a slasher in a horror movie. For the first time in years, I feel something! She makes me feel something. Heat. Light. Electricity. Magnetism. The fundamental forces that shape the fabric of the universe are condensed and pressed into this woman who stops me in my tracks.

I start weaning off the pills and cheating on Anna and spending more and more time in San Fernando Valley in the company of people who are fearlessly and unabashedly themselves. I am angry all over underneath and they tell me it's okay. I am repressed, stifled, and still so painfully shy and they show me another way. I am a bottomless well of sadness, so heavy with the collected sorrow of my lifetime that I fear I will not survive it. But they take me in, they absorb my burden, they make me their family and in their fucked up, dysfunctional way, they return me to myself. They make me see, once and for all, that our differences are weapons. Our dark has immense power.

This pornstar calls herself Margot. Her real name is Isla. I'm not supposed to ever tell anyone that, but I feel like we're having a bit of a breakthrough here, so let's keep it between us, okay? She really gums up the works, you know? Anna leaves me, my agent worries over her fifteen percent, there are some ugly scenes with the paparazzi, and the rumor mill starts spewing the nonsense that sells tabloids. My entire dazed, anesthetized rise to the top of the anthill is looking pretty precarious right now and I honestly can't tell you if I'm going to survive in Hollywood for much longer. But I'm alive, Dad. For the first time in my entire life, I feel every fucking thing inside of me.

Margot believes that the minute I accept who I am, the

bullshit and the real, the good and the bad, and that I cannot be one without the other, I will be unstoppable. I don't know if I'm there yet. To be fair, I don't know if I ever will be. But she's made me brave enough at least to tell you this: I love you, Dad. I love you and it breaks me to sit here and not even know if I'm just talking to myself. I don't know if there's anything left of you in there. But if you're in there somewhere, if you can hear me, I love you.

I feel like I waited too long with us and I'm sorry. It's always been so hard to talk to you. To just sit and talk to you. I have people I can sit and bullshit with for hours on end about everything from new shoes to faces in clouds. I can walk into a room and strike up a conversation with just about anyone, the one true dividend-paying gift of being a veteran of the service industry. But with you it's like pulling teeth. The silences, those awful silences where I feel like I'm going to climb out of my skin and shriek, I hate them. I always hated sports and we never had overlapping interests. I never learned how to bridge that gulf between us, and that is my greatest regret in this life. Just to shoot the shit with you, man, without the weight of all we cannot say in our silences. That's all I ever wanted for us.

Anya tells me that just being there is enough. That in the end, when God or whoever judges us, it will not be the quality of our words, but the quality of the time we spent that will matter. I don't care about God judging me, but I can't deal with the thought of you hating me because I didn't try hard enough. I tried though, Dad. Fuck, I try every day. Is that enough? Is it enough that I don't completely throw myself into self-destruction? Is it enough that your reward for being a good parent is me sparing you a grisly end and a terrible phone call in the middle of the night? Is it enough that I distance myself only to protect you from the sight of my unstoppable, unbearable, unapologetic darkness? Is it enough that I can't talk to you because I really don't have anything to say beyond I love you and you know that many times over by now?

When I was a teenager, I rebelled against you. When I was a young man, I used you like an ATM machine. As an adult, I ran from you because I couldn't bear to see the man I lionized for so long shrink and stoop with age and sickness. I just couldn't take anymore sadness, Dad. Do you see that? Do you get that? Tildie broke my heart. She broke my heart, beyond repair. I can still hear her screaming at night and I remember swabbing her cracked lips and turning her for bedsores and the cesspool stench that rose from her insides when she coughed. I can't do it. I can't do any more. It's not you. Please know that. It has never ever been because of you. I am torn apart because I feel like I've abandoned you when you needed me most. I turned my back and I ran for the hills while you slowly lost your mind and everyone took on that burden except for me.

But I live for you regardless. I live through you and because of you and more and more of you carries me forward as I get older. The only thing that remotely resembles a moral compass in me has come from you and when you are gone, the transformation will continue until one day I am you, and everything will have come full circle. I am better because of you and I am diminished by the reality of you dying here in this terrible place in this godawful town. Thank you for everything. Thank you for every single thing you've ever done for me.

I know your biggest worry has always been me. Anya was born responsible and dutiful and the kids are all carbon copies of her. Mom is a rock. And even Ted is dependable in the same way you can count on strays to come calling for food. I'm the wildcard, I get it. These days I'm trying to own it. But I want you to know I'm okay. I mean it, I'm okay. You don't have to worry about me anymore. I'm in choppy waters in a rowboat with a big assed hole in the bottom and I'm bailing, baby. I am bailing like my life depends on, because it does. But Arthur, I'm going to be okay. We're all going to be okay. I promise.

You can go, Dad. Tildie's waiting for you. And you know how impatient she gets…

* * *

Ronan was crying, leaned over the bed rail, both his hands wrapped tightly around Arthur's. He didn't feel any of the peace or sense of things set right they harped on in all those Hallmark movies. No beams of light broke through the gloom to halo the old man's head and the soaring choir of cherubs never materialized. He felt neither lighter nor saner having unburdened himself and that sense of completion he longed for so badly was nowhere to be found. He didn't expect to be doing cartwheels down the halls of the ICU, but he expected more somehow, some last push that clicked the odometer over and told him he'd gone somewhere. A journey was taken, an era was passing, the weather was changing. An end was coming. A life was drawing to a close.

From the bedside, Ronan felt his father's fingers, at first a slight shake, only the faintest trembling and he had to convince himself he was actually feeling something. But then, a squeeze, definitive, unmistakably Arthur. Ronan squeezed back, faith unfurling in him for the first time that somewhere under all the sedation, from some safe central place in the labyrinth of his mind, his dad, for however long they had left, was still in there somewhere.

And that he had heard him.

Chapter Fourteen

Twelve hours later, the call came. After a knock down, drag out battle with Anya and Ted over dinner -

He won't go to heaven if he kills himself.

This is what you're worried about right now? He's still alive, Anya.

'We are stewards, not owners, of the life God has entrusted to us. It is not ours to dispose of'

This right here is every single thing that's wrong with your religion. The kid needs help now, not in the fucking afterlife.

Language.

Fuck yourself, Ted.

-he retreated to his room, fuming. The kids followed shortly after, Ruth armed with a plateful of desserts and Benji with his deck of Uno cards. The game began listlessly, but soon they were laughing and teasing each other and tension started to lift. The mood in the room was approaching joyful, but Ronan was still worrying over his oldest nephew and preparing himself for a visit to see him in the hospital, flagrantly against the wishes of Joel's parents. He wanted eyes on the kid. All he had to go on was coming from Sister Anya and the holy rollers and was suspect by default. He had pieced more together from the kids, but even they didn't really understand what was going on in Joel's head. Headspace was like real estate and real estate was about one thing: location, location, location. Where was the kid's headspace right now? Because the very color of the territory he was looking out onto was dependent on that key piece of real estate between his ears.

Ronan was far from a psychologist and he was a poor therapist, even to his closest friends, but he knew human behavior with an instinct that bordered on supernatural. He could size up situations and people pretty quickly and he was right often enough that he came to rely on his powers of observation.

The last time he'd seen Joel was six years ago; he was eleven. Anya had come out for Christmas with the kids. Ruth and Benji were still little. It was a total surprise and she came without Ted, another surprise. It was the closest she'd ever come to leaving him and that week had been a tense one. Joel, even then, was a serious kid, far more sensitive and deep than the others. He'd taken to Ronan and the two of them explored LA and bonded as best as distant family can. But one good week in ten years did not qualify Ronan to evaluate what was going on now. He feared he was overstepping his bounds, even as he was actively planning on doing just that. Did he have any rights getting involved? Did an absentee uncle who never made an effort to be in touch with his family have any say or sway in what was unfolding in Joel's life? Maybe he should just keep out of it and-

I can't! Okay. I can't. I waited too long with Dad. I own that. But I can't just do nothing this time. I can't let this kid end up in a tub with a needle in his arm.

Anya was at the door. The look on her face drained the

levity out of the room. She held her phone at her side, her hand was shaking. She looked at Ronan.

"It's mom," she said. "Dad's gone."

She stepped into the room and the kids got up. She reached for them and held them while they started to cry. She stretched her arm out to Ronan, but a switch had been tripped. He had been activated. Something snapped loudly in his mind and he was summoned into action. He took his coat off the chair and his keys from the night table.

"Ronan!" she called.

He moved past her without a word, bounding down the stairs two at a time, keys clutched tightly in his fist.

"Ronan!" She shouted. "Where are you going?"

He slammed the front door hard enough to shake the whole house and half ran down the driveway. He got into the car and revved the engine, pulling out of the drive with a squeal of tires, flying down to the end of their street like a man on fire. He pulled out into traffic and was on the highway doing 90 before he fully realized what he was doing. He didn't even know what he was going to say to Joel when he got to the hospital, but he was certain that whatever transpired from this moment forward, it was his father's doing.

* * *

"It's after hours, Mr. Besso," the nurse told him. "This is highly irregular."

She looked tired. The harsh fluorescents cast her in a deathly green pallor and even the starched white of her uniform looked dingy under the lights. The lines of her face were stark, harshly drawn by the constant fake daylight customary in every sallow place like this that had ever been built. This was not the flattering lights of a movie set - no key light, reflectors, or soft boxes here - this was a utilitarian location where the only warm glow came at the end of a hypodermic needle.

Ronan debated bribery; he had a few hundred bucks in his wallet. Or threats. They were never his strong suit and a tactic he only deployed when every other avenue had been thoroughly exhausted. His star power, whatever of it there was in a place like this, was dubious and unlikely to wave him through any locked doors. In the end, he chose honesty, another tactic he rarely deployed, but seemed the only option available to him in the moment.

"Look," he said. "His grandfather just died. No one's going to tell him. You get me? They're just going to let him sit in here unaware that he's just lost someone who loved him."

She considered him, softening the slightest amount.

"Why aren't his parents here to tell him?"

"They sent me," he said quickly - a lie, granted, but in the spirit of the truth, at least.

She frowned, looking down at Joel's chart. Ronan doubted his name was on the contact list. He followed up quickly.

"They have two other children, Benji is still small. They've got my mom to deal with. It's kind of a cluster right now."

Her hand hovered over a plastic bin with blank tags in it. She locked eyes with Ronan, trying to sum him up. She closed her eyes a moment, a decision reached, and then fished a visitor pass out of the bin and passed it to him.

"He's up and in the common room," she said. "We'll bring him to intake. You can wait there while we get him."

"Thank you."

"You can't take him out on the grounds after dark and you can't leave anything with him."

"Okay."

"Through the doors past me on the left. A guard will search you and show you in. You'll be searched again on the way out."

"Okay, thank you."

He took the pass and clipped it to the lapel of his jacket.

"Mr. Besso?"

He turned.

"I'm sorry for your loss."

It was the first time he'd heard it, the first time the words had been spoken in his presence. He felt a massed and pressured wall of grief move against the dam of his self control. He forced himself to breathe and keep it together; a breakdown here wouldn't do anyone any good. He gave the woman a nod and attempted what he could muster as a smile. He moved through the double doors to security and got ready to see his nephew.

∗ ∗ ∗

Joel was tall - *God, he got so tall!* - but he walked with his head and shoulders stooped. His mop of sandy brown hair hung in his face and he looked like an amiable sheep dog. His green eyes, Anya's eyes, a wondrous chemical reaction between his father's deep brown and his mother's pale blue, were shrewd and alert. They were ringed with dark circles and Ronan could see the collected marks of hard travel etched into his face. He was older now than his seventeen years, older by far. He wore gray sweatpants, hospital slippers, and a white tee shirt that was about two sizes too big for him. Above the neck of his shirt, Ronan could see the hectic, healing bruises, still swollen and colored an ugly mix of blue and red and purple.

Joel hugged him, reluctantly at first, as if fearful of his own strength, and then with an appreciation of contact that only comes after a long time of not being touched. They parted and Ronan held his shoulders, looking at him, trying to see past him to decipher what was hiding underneath.

"Damn, it's good to see you, kid."

Joel shrugged and gave a half smile. Ronan released him and they sat side by side against the long table in the intake room. Outside, a plump orderly thumbed through a magazine, glancing in at them from time to time. It felt like a fishbowl.

"What are you doing here, Uncle Ronan?"

Ronan did his very best not to cringe away from Joel's voice. It was scratchy and tortured, the Marlboro man meets a kid whose voice is just starting to change. He hoped he hadn't betrayed anything, but the shock of it pained him. He'd crushed his vocal cords of course. Ronan forced himself to speak.

"What? I can't come see my favorite nephew when I'm in town?"

The casual tone was a mistake. Ronan saw the first glint of steel come into Joel's eyes. The boy crossed his arms over his chest.

"You know Benji might still buy that favorite nephew stuff, but I'm not that gullible anymore."

Ronan looked him over.

"No Joel, I suspect you're not. I apologize."

"Don't you have better things to do? I figured you'd be in LA doing another big special for TV or something."

"No one told you I was coming?"

Joel shook his head.

"No one tells me anything in here."

Ronan changed tactics.

"Are they treating you okay?"

Joel shrugged and stared at the orderly outside, avoiding eye contact.

"I guess," he murmured.

"Do you need anything?"

Joel turned and stared at him with a look so insatiate, Ronan felt his skin crawl.

"Got any dope?"

"Fresh out," he said, meeting Joel's eyes with some steel of his own.

"Shame."

The clock on the wall ticked, loud in the quiet room. The seconds passing were the only sound for a long while.

"What happened, Joel? Can you tell me?"

The boy laughed then, a supremely bitter thing, made metallic, almost robotic coming from his ruined throat. He touched his bruises and looked up into the corner of the room.

"I wanted to go to New York City with some friends. Mom wouldn't let me go. I've never been, you know? It wasn't just that, but that was kind of the last straw. I tried to end it, the rope broke."

Ronan's eyes widened.

"I know, it's one of mom's miracles, right? Even better than Christ on a piece of toast, isn't it?"

He laughed again, the wheezy rattle of a tired old smoker.

"I was unconscious when I dropped. Ruth found me. My folks were out. She went hollering around to the neighbors and someone called an ambulance. I woke up here."

He squeezed his hand around his throat. He winced, it looked like it hurt, and Ronan was about to stop him, but something in the boy's gaze kept him pinned to his chair.

"Much to my dissatisfaction."

"Jesus, Joel."

Joel rotated his neck in a half circle, first one way, then the other.

"Figured you'd roll up in here on your high horse and gimme a pep talk, right?"

Ronan made to protest, but Joel cut him off.

"Buck up, kid, it's not so bad! Right? Make yourself feel a little better that you finally did your civic duty after ten years?"

"That's not fair."

Joel laughed, healthier this time, made rich from anger.

"No? You think I'm the same kid who thought you were the shit because you took me to some cool places when we came to visit you? Then what? Cards? Cash on holidays? What else? Where were you, Uncle Ronan? You weren't even there when I was born! We had to come to you! Look at me! You don't even know me. You just ran away from us, from my mom, from Nonna and Nonno. You turned your back on us and now you think you have something to say because you're famous?"

"Joel, that's enough."

"Well I've got something to say, and it's from me and my whole family. Fuck you, Uncle Ronan."

"Joel-"

"Get out of here. And don't ever come back."

"Nonno is dead."

Joel shut his mouth with a snap. He deflated, the anger flagging, his body caving in, stooped shoulders returning. The ice in his eyes thawed and he blinked.

"What?"

"They weren't going to tell you, but I thought you should know."

"I-"

"I don't know when the services are going to be, but you're going to be there. I'm going to see if I can talk your folks into a temporary bereavement release or something."

"Uncle Ronan, I-"

Ronan stuck a finger in his face.

"You want to check out, you'll get no pep talks from me. But you're going to see what a real funeral for a great man looks like before you go preparing your own."

Ronan got up from his chair and tapped the glass. The guard looked up and approached the door with a set of keys. Ronan left the room without a look back and marched back out through security and reception to the parking lot. Shaking, he lit a cigarette and smoked it all the way down to the filter. When he felt like he could drive, he guided the car off the grounds and back towards home. He got through three lights before the tears came and he pulled over, sobbing, hammering on the steering wheel with his fist, screaming, already missing his father.

Chapter Fifteen

*D*ear Ronan,

*I dreamed about you. I dreamed we were Thelma and Loui-
seing it down some desert highway with the cops chasing us. You
were driving like a demon and I was singing, if you can believe
that. I think it was some old school Patsy Cline, but it's fuzzy
now and I can't be sure. But you were YOU. The you only I can
see right now, but the you everyone will see before too long.*

*You were sharp and keen and your edges whistled when you
moved through the air, the whistling tang of a hero's weapon
unsheathed. Your posture was erect and your eyes brimmed with a
look past morality, past mortal concerns - way past the limitations
that have imprisoned you for so long. You were actualized. A
Ronin of old. No master. No house to serve. Amassed with the
lifelong skills of a killer, you stalked the world of my dreams like
a giant of Jotunheim and the ground quaked as you passed over.*

You were immaculate.

*That scares me, you know. I won't be able to keep you much
longer. Soon my work with you will be done and you'll be ready
to leave me. I know I will hammer you and fold you and forge
you in a furnace so hot it fuses your atoms to impossible hardness
and tempers you into the man I see beneath your facade. I will*

dip you lovingly in water and drink of your steam like ambrosia. I will tend you while you cool and polish you until your blade gleams bright like a mirror. I will craft your guard, grip, and pommel and carve a sheath from the tallest tree in my forest. I will cut off my locks, dip them in resin and wax, and braid them into a fine baldric. As a final offering to you, I will run that blade across my palm and bleed into it, the first stain on your perfect instrument. Your first cut. The only blood you will ever spill that is given freely to you. I will wash you with the very force that pumps through my veins. I will bathe you so all you ever see again is red.

Selfishly, perhaps covetously, I will place you on an ornate shelf in my memory palace. I will use my method of loci to build you a palatial antechamber that is only for you, far from the stuffed hides and trophies of the boys who came before. I will sit in a leather lounge chair and spread my legs and soak my panties and make myself scream and tremble at the thought of you cutting me to ribbons. I will worship you, resisting running myself completely through you solely because you will it. I will submit to you, my Ronin, because you will be the finest creation that I have ever made.

But I can't keep you, can I? A weapon like you is to be used, not left idle on a shelf, gathering dust. Weapons are not art. They can surely be artful, but they are not art. They are built for a grim and practical duty. Forged by necessity, they do not hang in galleries and studios, they live and come alive on the blood-soaked fields of battle. And you are needed. Believe it. Know it to be true. The world needs you more than I do.

It needs you to be sharp and direct. It needs you to be unforgiving and to make unforgiving cuts. It needs your mind and your observation and the keen intelligence that made me even deign to look at you in the first place. It needs you to wake them up. They are sleeping, a slumber so deep and so thorough, they don't even know they're dreaming. They sleepwalk towards destruction. They Wile-E-Coyote their way off the cliff and they can't see that the moment they look down, it's freefall. Collapse. The bottom falls out. The center will not hold.

We all burn on re-entry.

I don't really like being touched. Did you know that? Did I ever tell you? I know that's quite a statement coming from a woman in my profession. When I know it's coming, it's okay. But even then, I can only take so much. If you ever saw me after a scene, I don't let any of the actors come near me. If you ever watch me in public, I position myself carefully with something between me - a desk, a table, whatever - so I can avoid it. Strangers touch me hesitantly, with clammy hands, like a button they were told not to futz with and can't resist putting their grimy little paws all over. And every actor I've ever worked with has been too rough. They grab, they don't touch. They dominate, they don't communicate - do you see the distinction? Some women like that, don't get me wrong, but not all the time. Certainly not as the default setting.

You're one of the very few who I really like it when they touch me. You touch me like a blind man. You see me with your hands. Every thing you want to say, you say with your hands. They are warm and strong and sure and my skin yearns for them. You will be rough with me when I demand it, but your default setting is firm and certain. You aren't milquetoast or unsure, like the trembling, sweaty, mother's basement, funk under the fingernails, stink fingers of the civilians reaching out for me at conventions. You touch me with urgency and something that borders on reverence. You touch me like you may never see me again and you must memorize me with your hands before you go.

You touch me this way because you were forged from kindness. Long before I got my claws into you, you were fully formed with a bomb-proof foundation of decency. I know men, Ronan. Trust me, I know just about everything there is to know about men. Good ones are more rare than Astatine (from the Greek - Astatos - meaning unstable. A delicious irony, no?). Good ones who aren't pussies or pushovers or mama's boys or weak when it counts or crushed by the weight of the inner turmoil of holding fast to the good in a world spun by commerce are even more rare. Good ones who remain good after life grinds them down again and again are statistically impossible. You are a bona fide rare earth element and I covet you. God dammit, do I covet you.

You will take my power and cherish these gifts I've given you and you will rise because of them. But you will never become a megalomaniac or a despot. Your foundation is rock solid and as sure and certain as the way you touch me. You are unassailable. Incorruptible. For the longest time I thought you were the best liar I've ever met. I convinced myself that you couldn't possibly be this real and it not be an act. I was positive you must have a stack of ruthlessly violated bodies under your cellar or a rich history of date rape under your belt. At the very least, a hateful past and a violent origin story.

You are no innocent. I've seen to that. Soundly. And proudly, I will admit. You're no bongo-banging hippie either, shaking your rose quartz and humming to attune your chakras, wide-eyed and trusting in some divine feminine superwomb to protect your delicate manic pixie dreams. Life has seen to that. Thankfully.

You are a perfect vehicle. Uniquely suited to walk us all into a new world. I told you once I saw a king in you, my darling. I have never deviated from that conviction.

You are close now. Hear me. You are close. This entire missive is a roundabout way of me telling you that I'm proud of you. You know I don't do the warm and fuzzy. I'm not built for it and it doesn't suit me to lie. Deal with your shit like a grown up and come to me to fuck and take drugs and to escape the drag of this mundane whirlpool. Go to your momma or your sidechick for milk and cookies and to suck on the big, swinging tit of make it all better. Don't waste my time with your weakness. I know the rules of vampires. I have to invite you in and you are not invited across my threshold so you can suck the energy from me to fill your own dreadful hollow. I deal with pretend and potential, the gritty grime of it is all on you. But I can manage to be proud of you. That I can muster without dying into you a little and losing myself.

When my mother died (cirrhosis of the liver, alone in a state hospital in Flagstaff, Arizona), I rented a fast convertible and drove eight hours from the valley to pull my pants down in broad daylight and piss on her grave. Then I took a can of gas out into the desert and I burned her trailer to the ground. I remember driving back to Cali, crying and laughing at the same time, the stink of gasoline still wafting off my hands. I was free then. Free like you are now.

You are handling your shit. You are doing what you need to do for your family. You are unapologetic and unafraid and your nephew can no doubt see the change in you better than the others. He'll come around, but he's yours now. Know that. Understand what that means if you can. We don't talk about this, because it frightens you when I do it and I do it enough for you to question your reality, but I am psychic. And you know well enough it's not in a playacting, made-by-Hasbro Ouija board, speaking in tongues, let's-fleece-the-Salem-tourists kind of way either. I see far, Ronan. I see all the way to the end on this one. You are close to assuming the throne.

You are one bold move away. I can't say more than that because even by saying it, I start to influence the outcome. But you will know it when it presents itself. You will know it and you will seize it. The kindest weapon ever forged will finally know its purpose. From there, you will not deviate. When that happens? You will step out and meet your audience at last, and I will be there waiting. You may hold no claim to my body or my heart or my soul, but I promise you, Ronan. Sealed with a kiss.

I will be waiting for you.

Lovingly,

Margot

Chapter Sixteen

The week went by in a blur. Many of Arthur's wishes for his arrangements had been planned well in advance and the rest boiled down to a series of increasingly uncomfortable meetings. There was procuring a death certificate, picking out a casket (Ronan added a new racket to his list, sliding caskets above flowers and cakes), talking with a mason about the headstone, and working out the details with Katherine's church and the funeral home.

It was a procession of serious faces, somber suits, and lowered voices in quiet rooms. The look was universal, as if more than practiced, somehow genetically inherent, programmed into the human animal in the face of grief. It was sanitized, whitewashed of the anger and outrage that rightfully accompanies loss. What remained was the placid acceptance of a great wheel turning, destined to crush all under its weight with time. There was understanding, a universal empathy. Who among us has not been touched by death? There were smiles, neither joyful, nor pitying, but patronizing and damnably patient.

It was all an act.

A natural performer, Ronan saw it clearer than anyone, though he suspected Ruth was bright enough to at least notice the strings of the puppets in the puppet show. Suddenly everyone had been Arthur's friend. Suddenly everyone wanted to know what they could do. Suddenly everyone was there (*No matter what!*) if and when you needed them. They were drawn to the corpse like flies, these sudden charlatans, eager to feast and lay eggs and propagate until the next corpse drew them onward. It sickened him. They reminded him of the crowd in that Ray Bradbury story, closing in, suffocating you with their curiosity, killing you as they closed their ranks.

It wasn't war stories and plates of hot casserole or sweating cocktails with moving toasts from a town come to pay its respects. Not yet. That parade would come later. This was the stuff of duty, the kind of thing done simply to come through the other side in order to begin the real work of unpacking bereavement. In Ronan's mind, those days to come were the hard ones. When it was finally time to empty their closet of clothes, donate precious mementos to Goodwill after the family had picked through all the choice items for themselves. When there was a terrible, lingering silence, those were the hard days. You'd wake from a fitful sleep and realize they were gone, set an extra place at the dinner table by mistake, or turn to talk to them in the car to find an empty seat. There was a person-sized hole that remained, even as reality rushed in to plug the vacuum, long after the casseroles and the sympathy cards had stopped coming.

This practical period, consisting of the logistics to move a dead body from the morgue to the earth, was done mostly on autopilot. Anya had taken on the role, bursting out of the gate unchallenged, turning all her force and focus on the somber set of tasks at hand. Ronan, sensing she needed purpose and control over this small, gloomy set of burdens, backed off and let her take the reigns. He spent most of his time consoling his mother, entertaining the kids, and avoiding Ted whenever possible. Ted, for his part, was quiet and respectful and did his best to fade into the background while the family buzzed around him. He kept his children clothed and showered and fed and stepped up behind the scenes in a way Ronan grudgingly admired.

Not that there wasn't a battle.

You had no right to tell Joel.

I had every right to tell Joel.

We're trying to protect him right now.

From what? Life? Stop treating him like he's made of glass.

He's just a boy.

Not anymore, he's not. Not by a long shot.

Ronan had spoken to both Joel's counselor and the attending physician at the hospital about a bereavement pass. Joel's counselor thought it would do more harm than good keeping him from his grandfather's services, but the attending physician disagreed. *In his current state, being face-to-face with mortality and the death of a loved one could trigger another suicide attempt,* he argued. Ronan skillfully pitted them against each other until they coughed up the paperwork for a temporary release. A decision would be reached, but only after receiving the signatures of both parents. Ted and Anya outright refused. *He's there for a reason, Ronan. People far smarter than you are in charge now. We're not going to rock the boat.*

He was undeterred. He managed to sneak away twice during the week to visit his nephew and each time the ice between them melted a bit more. At night, when everyone was asleep, Ronan rooted around Anya's house, digging through her makeshift office in the basement for legal paperwork or mortgage documents to lift their signatures. Pleased with his forgery, tickled by his treachery, he returned to the hospital and fed them some classic Ronan Besso bullshit about how he was in charge of all this funny business because funeral arrangements and familial duties were consuming all of his poor sister's and brother-in-law's energy. Perhaps because of his persistence, or the skill of his lies, or the results of an overburdened, underfunded and largely indifferent system, Joel's leave was approved two days before the funeral.

Ronan was rolling some big dice and he was keenly aware of it. He couldn't predict how seeing his grandfather dead in a box would affect his nephew. He had no way of knowing if it wouldn't inflict more damage, or add to his trauma, or trigger him into despair. He knew he was likely being naive, possibly selfish, and that he was grossly violating the edicts of a time-honored system put in place to mitigate the risk of another suicide attempt. But he also knew, in a part of himself that he was only recently coming to trust, that Joel would never get over missing his grandfather's funeral.

For Ronan, that was all he needed.

* * *

"Oh, I don't know," Katherine said to him.

The suit lay across the big bed. It was a sharp navy blue with faint gray pin striping; Arthur's court killer suit, his favorite. She had picked out a bright white poplin shirt to go with it, but she was fussing over the tie. In her left hand, she held a traditional red power tie, the kind of red you saw on the ribbons of war medals or royal sashes. In her right hand, she held a blue tie, a light azure. It was woolen and had a rich texture to it that drew the eye.

"I like the blue, Ma."

She lay the blue tie over the suit, folding it under the collar of the shirt and wrapping the sport jacket around it. She worked at her lip with her free hand, tugging and frowning.

"I don't know," she said. "The red has authority."

The man is dead, Ma. Who's he got to impress at this point?

"But the blue is peaceful. Restful. You feel me?"

She nodded.

"I feel you," she said slowly, the expression alien in her mouth. "But…"

"What would Dad do in this situation?"

She played with the lapels of the suit and smiled to herself.

"He'd be mad at all this fanfare. He wanted to be cremated."

That makes two of us.

"I know what he'd do," Ronan said and took a quarter from a small pile of change on the nightstand. "He'd make us flip for it."

"'If one is truly indifferent to or uncertain of the outcome…'" she began.

"'Then an unaffiliated third party is a welcome mediator,'" he finished.

She reached for his hand, covering it with her own.

"He loved you so much, Ronan."

"I know he did, Ma."

"He was so proud of you."

Ronan was suddenly embarrassed.

"I don't know about all that."

Katherine lay the red tie down next to the other one and sat down on the bed. She patted the place next to her and gestured to him.

"Come sit with me."

Clutching the quarter tightly in his hand like a talisman, Ronan sat down beside her.

"Your father always believed in you-"

"Come on, you don't have to do this-"

"Listen to me now, will you?"

He meant to press on, but he knew the look on her face from childhood. Katherine meant to have her say.

"Do you remember when you were a teenager? You kept all those journals? You wrote stories and observations and the very first of your jokes in those books. You carried them around everywhere!"

Ronan remembered, those books were a lifeline at that age.

"Your father read one once. You left it in the living room and he picked it up."

"You read my journals?"

"Of course we did, Ronan, we're your parents. You think we didn't know about the stack of girly magazines under your mattress or the marijuana cigarettes you used to hide in Anya's music box?"

He laughed.

"Busted," she teased.

"So Dad spied on me to make sure I wasn't a serial killer writing manifestos, is that what you're telling me?"

She looked at him, shocked.

"No honey. He spied on you because he was trying to *know you.*"

The words hit him, straight through to his heart. He never knew his dad to be that way, curious about his life or who he was as a person. It touched him.

Why didn't you ask me? I would have told you. Christ, I would have told you everything.

"He came up to the bedroom and he read to me. He read the whole thing, cover to cover. He was amazed with your vocabulary, your command of the language, how you seemed wise beyond your years. He was so impressed with how funny you were. Ronan, he was star struck! I mean it."

Ronan felt a lump in his throat. He swallowed and had to close his eyes a moment.

"But he was scared for you. I remember."

Ronan turned to look at her.

"What do you mean?"

"He was terrified you were so far beyond him, beyond us, that he wouldn't be able to advise you. He knew the law and the ways and means of carving out a regular, if moderately privileged life. You were something altogether foreign to him. He could see your talent, even then, and he worried over you. He didn't know how to help you navigate it or how to plot a way forward for you. But he was certain. You were going to be a name in lights one day."

"Mom, I…"

"He knew it."

Then why didn't he say anything to me? How come-

"How come he never said anything?"

She touched his cheek, holding her hand there, studying him carefully.

"He did, Ronan. In so many small ways, he did."

It was like he had forgotten the sun was behind the clouds. For all this time, for all these years, he had taken the clouds his father projected to be the only truth in the sky. But the sun had always been shining behind them, hadn't it? Realization dawned. The clouds parted, and Ronan allowed himself for to bask fully in the warm yellow rays of his father's pride for the first time. His mother, seeing the realization root and take hold, leaned in and kissed him gently on the cheek.

"Let's go with the blue tie," she said.

She rose from the bed, decision made, and returned the red tie to its place on the rack in the closet. Ronan followed, pocketing the quarter, deciding to keep it as a reminder of the sun, understanding it had been a talisman all along.

* * *

Ronan brushed colored leaves off Matilda's grave. He pulled dead flowers out of weathered pots and debated taking the old pots with him to the trash. His mother, even after all these years, still brought fresh flowers. The sight of these dead ones told him just how bad things must have been for Katherine to let nature take over for so long. Ronan liked it a little overgrown like this, a little weathered. It reminded him more of a monument than a memorial. Matilda had long gone the way of myth and legend anyway. More and more he had trouble remembering her face.

There was a chip in the stone at the corner frame by her name. Ronan didn't know who to contact to fix such a thing and wondered if his mother would notice. The day was warm. There had been mist in the early morning that had burned off into a dry gold gift of Indian summer. The night would be crisp and Halloween lurked just around the corner. It was Ronan's favorite holiday. The last of summer and the best of fall rolled into one phantasmagorical night where the veil between worlds thins and nothing is quite what it seems. Fitting he was alone in a cemetery, prowling around his sister's derelict grave on a day at the death of the summer. It matched his mood.

He was exhausted. Not from lack of sleep or overwhelm from the week, but as one who is living raw through every single second of *life as it is* with no reprieve or escape. He was exhausted because he couldn't zone out or distract or hide. The week was burned in behind his eyes, so hot he could still see the afterimage when he closed his lids. He was, eyes wide, locked in, staring at the events taking place and it demanded all of his attention. It compelled him to look. He was paralyzed, tears streaming from the side of his open eyes because he couldn't look away from pain. He was either hurting or managing hurt somewhere else. It was a triage of loss. The pain, a noise in his head, was constant.

Matilda's stature in life and in Ronan's imagination when he talked to her, was small. She had been a child and then gone and he never let his imagination conjure what she may have aged into in the intervening years. Whether this came from laziness or reverence, he couldn't say, but her size, real and imaginary, invited sitting or kneeling, so as to be level with her. Ronan obliged her and set himself down in a patch of sun, cross-legged, next to her stone.

"Hi kid," he said. "It's been a while."

For a long time, he thought it was disrespectful to smoke

here, but age was knocking down norms left and right, and he chanced it. He had been smoking less since that first night he left Joel in the hospital. He was running one errand after another and any cigarette taken was a joyless suck to draw in as much free-radical gumbo as possible between appointments. He'd stab them out after a few puffs and then save the butt to light up again later. The butts reeked after this and he was disgusted with himself. He took his time now, savoring the peaceful ground and the quiet. Smoke drifted in spirals and leaves tumbled end over end among the rows of graves.

"I'm up to no good, Tildie," he said. "I'm going to spring the kid."

He smoked. He watched a hawk rise out of a tree and circle, then dive, talons out, closing in on a meal on the run.

"I need your blessing on this one."

The patch of sun he was sitting in darkened as a cloud passed over them. The chill in the breeze revealed itself in the shadow and distant tree branches swayed. Ronan sighed and nodded.

"I'm gonna do it anyway."

The wind breathed through the trees, sending leaves to scatter across the lawn.

"I know," he said.

The hawk screeched and rose into the air again, denied its prize, circling overhead, back to searching. The cloud moved on, sun rays breaking through its edges, shining down on Ronan and Matilda.

I know.

He took a last drag and stamped the cigarette out on the bottom of his shoe. He sat for a long while, remembering.

When at last he rose and dusted himself off, the light had changed. He lingered, brushing off leaves and tugging at overgrowth. Then he leaned down and tenderly kissed her stone and started the long walk back to the car.

Chapter Seventeen

He carried two cracked plastic pots and a small trellis back with him to the car. Bemused, he realized he didn't know how to open his trunk yet. He fumbled with his keys until he found the right button and the back popped up with a hiss. He leaned down to drop his handfuls and found a ribboned bottle of Krug and a card. He opened the envelope.

Dom Perignon is for rednecks.
Congrats on the new ride.

Kisses,

A.

P.S.. Drink some of this with your sister. You may be surprised what comes of it.

Trading pots for champagne, Ronan took the bottle to the front with him. He nestled it into the passenger seat and even made a show of fastening a seatbelt around it. He rang Anya.
"Hello brother."
"Hello sister."

"You're in a good mood."

He checked in with himself and found that he was.

"Will you have a drink with me?"

She laughed. It was tired, but it was genuine.

"Do I sound that bad?"

"You've sounded better. Come on, let's have a drink."

"Ronan, I can't. I have to drop Ruth over to-"

"Anya!" he shouted.

"Jesus, what?"

"Tildie says you have to."

She was silent a moment.

"That's where you are."

"'Give strong drink unto him that is ready to perish, and wine unto those that be of heavy hearts.'"

"Fine. Come over."

She ended the call. Ronan looked over to the bottle and patted its cork.

Okay Arlo, let's try it your way.

* * *

"You remember the time you guys had that scavenger hunt?"

Ronan refreshed her glass.

"You stole the Marlon's horse trailer-"

"We didn't know-"

"And who was it? Was it Fowler?"

Pink had risen in Anya's cheeks. She was talking with her hands.

"It was Fowler. He was so drunk, he let the horse out. Run free, Secretariat!"

She covered her mouth, spilling some of her champagne.

"Dad came home to the fire department trying to get this horse out of Bedelia Gellar's flowerbeds. He was *furious*."

"It didn't help you were throwing up Southern Comfort on the deck chairs."

She made a face and spat out her tongue.

"Oh, gross!"

"I think we're technically still grounded."

"I'm going to fuck up your planetary alignment!" she shouted, slamming her palm against the table, sending over the salt and pepper.

"Jesus. His temper," Ronan said, shaking his head.

"I'm going to count to three. If I get to four-"

"I'm gonna start throwing your toys out the goddamned window!" they shouted.

"Remember when he caught you kissing the Martino's kid?"

"Christian! Ugh!" she said. "He was worse than Southern Comfort."

"No daughter of mine is going to be entertaining peckers in this house!"

"Like I was setting out the good plates and making up the guest room."

"Welcome, peckers, to our lovely home!"

The laughed together, passing each other a look long absent. Anya's eyes gleamed, her hair loose and free around her shoulders. Her chill pallor was warming with the laughter and the half-empty bottle of Krug between them. Ted came down the stairs and wandered into the kitchen. He waved at them and walked to the fridge.

"Sorry to interrupt, I'm just grabbing a beer."

Ronan felt a stab of empathy and goodwill run through him. Unsure how long this strange new feeling would linger, he invited Ted to join them.

"Forget the beer, come have a glass of 400 dollar champagne."

Ted chanced a smile at Ronan.

"Can I do both?"

Ronan grinned.

"Ted, my man, go crazy."

Ted took two beers from the refrigerator and handed one to Ronan, settling himself down next to his wife. Ronan poured a flute for Ted and set it in front of him. He raised his own glass to them.

"To Arthur."

"To Arthur."

"Ted, did you know your wife used to be cool?"

Ted leaned into Anya, bumping her with his shoulder.

"I did not know that."

"She almost got us kicked out of a church once."

"Stop it!"

"This I have to hear."

"Stop it right now!"

"Overruled!"

He refreshed their glasses and took a long pull from his beer. It was delicious. He tipped his head to Ted.

"Our Great Aunt's funeral was at this super old-school Catholic megaplex and there was this frozen nun as a centerpiece at the altar."

Anya slapped Ronan's arm.

"She wasn't frozen. She died a Saint and she doesn't decompose. It's a miracle."

"Frozen nun," Ronan repeated. "Like a bug in amber."

Anya rolled her eyes.

"He wouldn't shut up about it."

"Are you kidding? I was, what? Ten? A frozen nun was better than fart jokes."

"The priest was trying to give the sermon and this one's asking me if they change her underwear or dust her on weekends."

Ronan took another drink and appealed to Ted.

"Oh, I had questions."

"We're cracking up in the back row and trying to hold it back, which you know only makes it so much worse."

"So the priest comes over and he's waving the incense and he walks back over to us and he leans over…"

"*It's time for you to get your shit together!*" Anya shouted.

She laughed hard, hugging Ted, spilling more champagne.

"He was so fucking scary, we shut right up and didn't say a peep for the rest of the service."

Anya closed her eyes and made prayer hands, then she was cracking up herself up again. Ronan rescued her glass from her elbow.

"Hey, watch it, this stuff is expensive."

She reached for the glass.

"Gimme that," she said and downed the remainder in one swallow.

She set the glass down on the table and nodded for another. She grinned.

"I'm still cool."

✳ ✳ ✳

"We're in major trouble for this, aren't we?" Joel asked.

He was changing out of his hospital sweats and into the suit Ronan had stashed in the back seat for him. Ronan drove, still checking the rearview mirror for many minutes after they escaped the hospital grounds.

"You? No. Me?" He sighed. "Oh yeah. Your folks are going to blow a gasket."

Joel buttoned his shirt, tucking it into his slacks haphazardly.

"What's the worst case?"

Ronan turned on him.

"No idea. I'm amazed we made it this far. I am improvving this whole gig at the moment. Just keep your head down and sit towards the back. Hopefully we can hide you until we get to the cemetery."

Joel nodded, fretting over the two ends of his tie.

"Do you know how to do one of these?"

Ronan passed him an annoyed look.

"Driving right now. Do a Tik-Tok for it. Christ."

Joel unlocked his phone and started scrolling. He stopped at a picture of a pretty blonde woman with heavy eye liner and big fake lashes. In one hand, she was holding the leash coming from a fuzzy pink collar around her neck. In the other, she held a gleaming metal butt plug to her wet-looking lips. She was naked, but for clogs, which for a reason quite beyond him, absolutely did it for Ronan.

"Thank you for bringing me my phone. Are you really dating Margot Throbbie?"

As if entertaining at one of his father's barbecues, Ronan asked, "Why? You know her?"

Joel's laughter filled the car. "Yeah man, I know her!"

"Joel, you dirty little dog."

He shrugged.

"I'm seventeen, man."

"You gonna give me shit?"

Joel shook his head.

"No way. I think it's epic," he said. "But, *how does that even work?*"

Ronan was thinking about clogs.

We are unfinished, Ronan. And I'm not done hating you yet.

And letters.

"Like, is she tired when she gets home from work?"

Ronan laughed despite himself.

"Fix your tie, fucker."

They drove to the church. Ronan parked towards the back behind a shuttle van, shadowed by a grove of trees. He smoked a cigarette while Joel finished with his tie. Ronan snuck looks at him, trying to figure out the mind of the boy next to him.

The shirt collar hid the marks and his voice was already stronger, but what was going on up there? They had to go in separately, there was no way around it. Would the kid just bolt when Ronan got out of the car and went inside? Even if he didn't, there was still no plan on how to get him out of there afterward. If the family got eyes on him, the pin was out of the grenade.

Lord graciously hear me…

"We meet back at the car afterward. If I'm not here, you wait. Yes?"

Joel nodded. Ronan stepped out of the car and walked toward the entrance. He climbed the stairs and entered the vestibule. He felt the feeling wash over him. It was always the same. In other cities. In other countries. Late at night and jetlagged and more than a little cocked on something. It didn't matter, there was always a feeling. It was automatic.

His chest expanded, his gait smoothed. He felt his spine lengthen with a satisfying pop. He felt his right hand at the ready, prepared to shake and cover and pat with sincerity. He set his expression to calm benevolence. He blinked a few times and brought forward into his eyes the patient, enduring expression of one shouldering a heavy burden.

His aunts. His uncle. His cousins. A smile for each of them. A few kind words. It always felt the same, working a room. It made him lighter, it made him joyful. He could pass through a wall of people on his way to the stage and give them the part of himself that he shed each time he was called to perform. From this place, this high-wattage setting, he could power city blocks for miles. They flocked to him, with hope in their eyes, reaching for him to receive a snatch of his light, taking it as sacrosanct, as they would take communion.

He worked his way to the front of the pews. His mother tapped her watch at him and slid over to let him sit beside her. He leaned over and nodded to Anya and Ted and the kids.

"We almost thought you weren't coming," she said.

"I'm here now."

"You look handsome."

"Thank you."

Katherine took his hand in hers and squeezed it to her leg.

"It's time."

"I'm ready."

Ronan risked a look behind him, but he couldn't find

Joel in the crowd. The priest and two altar boys approached the dais.

"Let us pray."

* * *

Ronan looked out into the crowd assembled in the church. He looked down to the casket on its wheeled stand - the guest of honor. The microphone, the same as all the ones in the clubs and bars that came before and unique here at the same time, smelled faintly of wine and that gave him a little smile. The professional emerged and he cleared his throat. His arms were easy at the sides of the podium and the shakiness in his stomach was gone.

He found Joel in the second to last row and nodded to him. Anya looked around, but it was too late to do anything about it now. He wasn't worried. A part of him could feel his father's hand gripping his own, sure and steady. He could hear the surf and feel the kind warmth of youthful summers on his face. He felt the waves swell. He cleared his throat a final time and jumped.

"'Stop all the clocks, cut off the telephone...'"

Chapter Eighteen

Towards the end of the service, he noticed two police officers standing in the vestibule. They watched the proceedings with their hands on their belts and made no move to intervene. Someone had squealed. Ronan had a good mind as to who it was, but Ted stared forward, seemingly oblivious to what was unfolding. He glanced at Anya, who was clutching her phone tightly to her side, lips pursed. She gave him a sorrowful look that stung of both admission and betrayal.

How could you, Ronan?

He guessed he shouldn't be surprised that Anya had made the call, but it hurt him nonetheless. He felt like they had crossed a gulf last night and that maybe some part of her understood there were things Ronan could do for the family that she could not. But he went behind her back, didn't he? He did it flagrantly, with a smile on his face, and to Anya that was a betrayal of its own.

He excused himself and walked over to the officers, trying to get a read on the situation before the hoopla ended and everyone broke for the cemetery. He approached them, stepping out into the vestibule and leading them away from the gathered mourners.

"Are you here to arrest me?"

The one to his left shook his head.

"No," he said. "You've got friends in high places. But Joel has to come with us."

Fowler.

Ronan pressed for more time. Whatever was unfolding here was, like so many other things in his life, unfinished. The ice was thawing with his nephew, but there was still a cloud hanging over him, and Ronan needed more from Joel before he'd let him go back to the hospital.

I don't think he really wants to die, but I need to be sure.

"Listen guys, I know this is a lot to ask, but can I deliver him after the burial? It'll be another hour at the max and I'll escort him to you personally when it's over."

Ronan could feel a manic energy surging through him and he wondered if what he said was even true. He pushed on.

"Let the kid bury his grandfather. Please."

The officers looked at each other. The policeman to his right, who hadn't yet spoken, looked into the church and then to Ronan.

"You have a choice to make," he said. "You can escort him out now or we can go in and get him. That's as far as the favors go today."

Ronan nodded and smiled at them in what he hoped passed for appreciation, but he felt the edges of his mouth hitch up a little too high and he wondered if he didn't look a bit unhinged. Things were breaking up inside and it was time to move. He thanked the officers, turning back inside to track down Joel and prepare for the second act.

* * *

"We have to go."

Joel looked to the vestibule, but saw it empty.

"Are they letting us go?"

Ronan grabbed his arm and started pushing him through the pew to the other side.

"No, they're just giving us a head start. Come on. We've got about five minutes."

What the fuck are you doing?

But he wasn't listening to the chorus anymore. He was driven forward by something else entirely now. His body was tense, but his heart was even in his chest and his palms were dry. He felt an overwhelming sense of deja vu, like this moment had happened a thousand times and each time the outcome had been the same. Deviation was impossible and he found he didn't want to stray from the path even if he had the option.

Was this fate? Was this what fate actually felt like? Stepping into a moment, knowing you have no other alternative, but also knowing, deep down in the way back of your mind, that every twist and turn and seemingly arbitrary choice you've ever made has led you to this singular occurrence.

"Side door. Go."

Anya was marching towards them, raising her voice, singling them out. People were looking now and he could see wide blue shoulders making their way into the church. Ted was moving parallel to his wife, trying to cut them off at the exit. Murmurs were rumbling through the crowd and Ronan could sense it all falling apart.

"Stop right there!" one of the cops shouted and the two barged their way through the pew.

"Run for it!" Ronan shouted and they bolted for the fire door.

Joel banged on the safety bar and the door flew open. They ran through into the sunshine, ties flapping in the wind. Joel was fast, long legs pumping like an Olympic runner, easily doubling the distance from Ronan as they sprinted for the car. Ronan found himself wondering if this wasn't the first time the kid had run from the cops.

Christ, I've got to quit smoking.

Then he was laughing. Amazed with himself, this only made him laugh harder. He was running full out, arms cutting through the air, trying to blink tears out of his eyes and howling like a loon as the car came into view. He pushed the remote starter on his key fob and the Caddy roared to life.

Thank you, Arlo.

Joel was already inside and pulling on his seatbelt. *Safety first!* Ronan thought crazily and the laughter made him shake so hard he feared he wouldn't be able to drive. But the minute he got behind the wheel, that fated directness took hold of him and he was in full command of his faculties. The voices rose again, urgent, frightened, the entire chorus utterly dependent on the next choices he made.

What the fuck are you doing?

But he knew. He knew down to the smallest detail.

* * *

Ronan sped past the turn for the cemetery. Joel craned his neck around, watching the turn fall behind them as they flew up the road.

"You're going to miss Nonno's funeral? Are you serious?"

"We made it to the service," Ronan said. "The rest is just a deposit."

Joel gawked at him.

"Look, I know where he's parked. He's not going anywhere. I'll visit him-

In five-to-ten, Ronan, my man. You are in deep shit.

-later."

Behind them, a police cruiser followed close behind, sirens blaring. It was quick cut through downtown and the park and then backroads to the highway. If he could get to the on-ramp, he could play this out on his own terms.

And then it's Staties and Staties don't play. They are going to seriously fuck up your planetary alignment.

"You really want to die, Joel?"

Joel opened his mouth to speak, but Ronan cut him off.

"Did you see Nonni when she gave her reading?"

"I-"

"Did you see your mom *lose her shit?*"

"It's not like-"

"Do you know what we lost today?"

"I'm sorry-"

"He was the best of us."

"I know."

"And he had a lifetime, Joel. You're just starting out. Who knows what you're going to see and do. Who knows what you could become."

"You don't know what it's like living there, Uncle Ronan. All they do is fight and-"

"You want Ruthie up there reading poetry for you?"

"No-"

"Or Benji?"

"I can't stand it!" Joel shouted, suddenly unleashing his fists on the dashboard, punching hard and fast, over and over until his knuckles split and bled. "I can't make it stop and I just need it to *stop*."

Ronan pushed down on the accelerator, running a red light and veering the car around slower drivers. The police kept pace with them, another cruiser barreling down the hill to join the chase. He could feel himself pushing Joel harder than he should, pushing the car too, perhaps himself most of all, but he couldn't stop that either.

"It never stops," Ronan said. "You just get better."

Joel nursed his knuckles, sucking at them, glaring side-eyed at Ronan.

"Everyone says it gets better."

Ronan punched the dashboard, hard, with his right hand. It surprised Joel and he shrank in his seat. Ronan pulled his hand back, his knuckles had broken open in three places. He flashed his hand at Joel in solidarity.

"Are you listening? I said *you* get better."

"Then what's the point?"

Ronan squeezed his hand into a fist and released it. The hot swollen ache in his knuckles felt like the best thing that had happened to him all day.

"There is no point, man. At least not one we could dream of understanding. This is just where we are and we have to look it in the face."

"That's easy for you to say. You get to go back to the sun and the girls and more money. I'm fucking stuck here."

"You want me to apologize for going for it? Good luck with that. I work for a living."

"Whatever."

"I'm still me, kid. No matter what my zip code says. I carry my shit *everywhere*. I live out there to protect you assholes. Someday you'll get what that really means."

A third cruiser had joined the fray and they were maybe two miles from the highway. Ronan peeked up at the rearview mirror, imagining what his mother's face looked like right about now. Anya must be apoplectic. There would be more cops waiting when he crossed into the next town and the State troopers might already be at the on-ramp depending on how quickly everyone got on the ball.

He snaked around a blue minivan and ran two more red lights. The on-ramp was a straight shot down a long stretch of country road that was all but empty at this time of day. Ronan pressed his foot further down and fields rushed by them.

"We're in this car until you tell me you don't want to die and I believe you."

Joel crossed his arms, sullen. He stared out his side mirror at the flashing lights.

"That's never going to happen."

"We'll see."

The on-ramp came into view. It was unguarded, unprotected. He pushed his foot all the way down to the floor. They pulled away from the pursuing officers and screamed onto the on-ramp like a pinball launched by a righteous shooter. The highway loomed, an asphalt raceway. Ronan was grinning and Joel was suddenly starting to see a fuller picture. The engine roared. The Caddy, a shining testament to good old-fashioned American engineering, hadn't even broken a sweat.

* * *

120 miles per hour. That was the fastest Ronan had ever driven in his life. In a rented Porsche on the 101 with Margot, one of their first official dates. She said she'd suck his cock if he put her in danger. Ronan felt like most women either smelled like flowers or fruit, but Margot smelled of spices from far flung foreign shores. It was like nothing he'd ever encountered before. She wanted danger and the scent of her drove him wild. Far more than blowjobs, Ronan wanted to imprint himself on this woman and drink of her. He whipped the Porsche forward and as red rose in her cheeks and her pupils dilated, it only got easier to speed.

"Do you want to die, Joel?"

The speedometer was approaching 140 and Ronan meant to bury the needle. Joel had one hand up against the dashboard and the other was gripping the side handle over his door. One knee was up, as if that would protect him from dreadful physics. The car was still accelerating.

"Answer me. Do you want to die?"

The highway was mostly clear. Any other cars blurred past in colored flashes. The forests and fields around them were a blended tapestry of Autumn colors. They cleared a bridge and an open stretch of highway opened before them. The police were following about a mile behind and seemed to be slowing. Whatever happened next, it would just be the two of them. The cabin was alive with the roar of the engine and they could feel the air pressure that was both trying to lift the car and keeping it firmly on the ground at the same time. The needle was buried. 160 miles per hour.

"Here's what going to happen," Ronan said, in a voice calmer than he'd ever spoken. "I'm going to take my hands off the wheel and we're going to kiss a guardrail or a pylon and we're going to end, son."

Joel reached up instinctively, but Ronan slapped his hands away.

"If you grab the wheel," he warned. "you'll overcorrect at this speed and we will flip, end over end, and just die faster."

Ronan relaxed his grip on the steering wheel. He looked over at his nephew.

"Did you know creativity and depression are lovers?"

And he let go.

* * *

In the years to follow, Joel would distance himself from Ronan. It would be a subconscious reaction, beyond both his understanding and his control. He would take a step back, believing himself to be giving his uncle respect and distance, but really to protect himself, removing himself as best he could from what he'd witnessed that afternoon on the highway.

He looked at Ronan, at the crest of the hill, car run to its red line, faster than he ever imagined. Cops chasing them. Palms barely touching the wheel. He was already prepared. He came this way, ready to do them both. Because if that's what Joel really wanted, who better to deliver him than someone who was unquestionably ready to go. Joel saw a death wish coloring his uncle's entire being. The wild eyes, the (extraordinary to think about, even years later) devil-may-care grin on his face and most alarming, the welcome expression on his face. This is what Ronan wanted. This is how he was built, from balls to bitten-down fingertips. Death. What Joel only dreamed of, what he fantasized about, worshipped and emboldened with his worship, was finally in the car with them and it terrified Joel in a primal place that shrieked in recognition and terror.

Joel was lost then, hurting in his own right and fully in the throes of hero worship. He was warmed by the attention of his uncle who truly and wholeheartedly seemed to give no fucks about anything. But the time after, time away, would cloud his vision and his image of Ronan as more alive wishing for death than any person he'd ever seen would fade and only a lingering unease would remain. Ronan had shown Joel his true face. And while Joel would admit, seriously and pointedly until his final moments, that his uncle put his own suffering in harsh perspective and likely saved his life, he had been full-on willing to kill them both to get there. His uncle had out-crazied him. This conveyed undying respect, but it would frighten him well into adulthood. A rift had formed and Joel would come to remember Ronan more and more as a cautionary tale.

* * *

"*I don't want to die!*" Joel screamed, curling himself into a ball in the passenger seat.

Ronan felt a longing moment, a moment that stretched

out and slowed to a yearning second of indecision, where he thought about ignoring Joel and letting the speeding car destroy them. He felt saliva fill his mouth and he could almost feel the lurch of the frame as the tires left the road. He could hear the first shrieks of metal and feel the devastating smash of impact, running through him so strongly, his flesh would liquefy and his bones would snap like dry winter twigs underfoot.

Let me join you and Tildie on a beach, Dad. It's all I've wanted. It's all I've wanted for so long.

"*Stop!*" Joel shrieked, voice high and tortured, breaking into sobs. "Please stop."

The moment passed. Ronan's hands returned to the wheel and his foot let up on the accelerator. The car slowed. He allowed himself to breathe, a great gulping swallow. The cabin was loud with Joel's crying and the rush of the wind. The police cars were closing and Fowler was calling in on the car's media center. There were other problems now, far more immediate. But the big one - Ronan looked over at his nephew, huddled and shaking in the seat beside him - the big one was resolved.

All the rest was the after party.

CHAPTER NINETEEN

Fowler calling.

Ronan took a breath and punched a button on the console. Even in the brief silence, he could hear Nate's anger coming through the car speakers.

"I told you I'd keep in touch."

"Lemme talk to Joel, Ronan."

Joel leaned forward. "I'm here, Detective Sergeant."

Of course he knows him. How many other favors has Fowler been doing for you over the years?

"Are you injured?"

"No, sir, we're both fine."

Breathing. Glowering. A motive force, alive in the speakers.

"I gave you a courtesy, Ronan."

"I know-"

"This is bad."

"How bad?"

"It gets worse the longer it goes on. I need you to pull the car over for me."

"So this is bad?"

Fowler barked into the phone, a sound that made Ronan jump, a rough approximation of laughter.

"Reckless endangerment. Kidnapping."

"Kidnapping?"

"This is bad. I could have helped you in town, but this is a problem now. You need to pull over or they will stop you."

Ronan gulped and he and Joel shared a look.

"They're not going to road spike us or shoot out our tires?"

"No, not while there's a minor in the car. They will road-block you and you won't be able to get around it and if you ram it, you'll put everyone's life in danger."

"Think we can make it to New York?"

That harsh bark came again.

"I don't think you'll make it to New Haven."

"Care to make it interesting?"

There was a long silence. Ronan thought he'd lost the call.

"You there?"

"You're doing this."

"I am."

Fowler took a breath. Ronan could picture him squeezing the bridge of his nose and clamping his eyes shut.

"Look, you have to slow it way down. You're putting people at risk. Do the speed limit."

"Like OJ?"

Another pause.

"You're being serious?"

"When they stop you, you get out of the car with your hands way the fuck up, Ronan. You're in a whole heap of trouble."

"Okay."

"Why are you doing this?"

"Does it matter?"

A final pause.

"For the record, no one shoots out tires. You really do live in the movies."

Fowler ended the call. The anger dissipated like a puff of smoke. Ronan set the cruise control for an even 70 and took his foot off the gas. About ten car lengths behind them, a line of police cars followed.

* * *

"How many do you count?"

Joel was leaned over the backseat, looking out the rear window. He had shed his jacket and tie and rolled up his shirtsleeves.

"I count five."

Ronan had remained suited. Something about the feel of being well-heeled calmed him. The big wheel was in motion now, at least he could introduce a bit of class into the recklessness.

Fowler is right. You do live in the movies.

"What now?"

Ronan looked at his nephew.

"You're not here against your will, are you?"

Joel turned back around in his seat and put his belt back on.

"Shit, no. This is your ass over the coals."

"So you're with me?"

"I'll bet Ruth is so jealous. Benji must be losing his shit."

Ronan looked in the rearview.

"Are you listening to me, Joel? This is important."

Joel nodded.

"I'm with you," he said. "I want to see how far we can get."

Ronan thumbed behind them.

"I've got a way we can get a lot farther than New Haven and guarantee we don't get fucking shot. But it's going to blow this thing up to boss level."

"And?"

Jesus, the kid is primed for destruction. You don't even need to ask.

No, but I need to hear it. For consent if nothing else.

"Are you with me?"

"Yes."

"I need to hear you say it."

"I'm with you."

Ronan pointed to the phone in Joel's lap.

"Look up tip-lines for the major networks. Start calling numbers until you get a real person and then hand the phone to me."

Joel held his hands suspended over his lap, uncertain in the moment.

"We'll be all over the six o'clock news."

Ronan nodded.

"This is your fifteen minutes if you want it."

Silence rose between them. It wasn't so much a battle of wills as it was forcing Joel to widen his scope beyond their immediate situation to see much larger pieces in motion. Joel understood his uncle was letting him make the choice for both of them. Ronan seemed prepared to meet his fate, however that might unfold. Joel knew if he asked him to pull over, that would be the end of it. Ronan would go to jail and he'd go back to the hospital and very little would have changed. This same scenario would also unfold if the word got out too.

But that middle part would be something else, wouldn't it? Maybe enough to change a lot of things.

Joel felt giddy. He felt a big-sky hugeness around him and he wanted to revel in it. The feeling of breaking out, breaking away, being legitimately *on the run*, flooded through him. It was so sudden, so novel, it threatened every sense of continuity he ever held. He felt paralysis spreading and knew the only way to counteract it was action. He took control of himself, for what felt like the first time, and brought the phone into his hands. He flicked the lock screen and then his hands were flying, eyes searching. Then the phone was pressed up against his ear. He was talking.

Behind them, the convoy was growing.

* * *

FaceTime call from Ma.

Ronan could picture her at the grave site, calling him while staring fretfully down at a mound of freshly dug up earth, sprinkled with flowers. Would they have gone through with the burial? He couldn't imagine they would hold something like that up, regardless of the circumstances. But this little stunt was something that couldn't be repaired with a hot plate of comfort food and TLC and he suspected deep down, his mother knew it too. This call wouldn't be accusatory; it was unlikely she'd even raise her voice. It would instead be dripping with worry and concern and the taint of what Margot would call, make-it-all-better. Somehow that was worse. He wanted hotness, outrage at ruining what was supposed to be a solemn afternoon and was fast turning into a full-on circus.

Hi, is this ABC? Great, this is Ronan Besso. Oh thank you, that's very kind of you to say, I appreciate it. Well, I'm calling because I'm currently in a police chase on interstate 95 in Connecticut. I have my underage nephew with me and we're trying to get to New York City. I thought, you know, maybe someone over there might want the scoop first. Sure I'll hold…

Ronan never understood people who would stick with the cult leader or the molesting priest or the Ponzi schemer when all their dirty secrets came to light. Piles of evidence and witnesses and whistleblowers and the fanatics still loved their guru, pouring money and misplaced worship into his coffers because they knew in their hearts their guy was innocent. It hurt Ronan's logic and his sense of propriety, yet his mother remained his number one fan, no matter what. He could feel her on the other end of the call, believing to herself that this was merely another merry prank on her son's madcap tour of the Northeast. Was that desperation? Was it love? Was it possible that the two were adjacent and on a long enough timeline, virtually indistinguishable from each other?

He couldn't bear the face of unconditional love. He didn't understand it and he didn't trust it. It was as alien a concept as multivariable calculus. It was possible he'd been out west too long or the steady assault of Margot's harsh philosophies had finally broken through, but he could understand transactional relationships. They made sense. Tit for tat. A for B. Scratch my back and all that. It's the ones who didn't want anything who made him uneasy. Someone who didn't want anything couldn't be leveraged or bought out or scared or threatened. They held all the power. Someone who loved you unconditionally? Well they invited the worst of you, didn't they? Because they had to prove it. You had to turn on them and bite them in order to see for yourself how much they really loved you.

Ronan knew he should take the call, especially today of all days. But he simply couldn't bear to look at his mother's face while he bit her. He let the call go to voicemail.

"She'll be all right," he said, more to himself than to Joel.

They drove on.

* * *

Anya Calling.

No FaceTime and make it all better from Anya. She was all business today. He was willing to bet she couldn't even look at his face without screaming and imagined this call would be a lot like trying to eat a plateful of broken glass. Under the Jesus Loves You smokescreen, Anya was a controlling micromanager who experienced black and decidedly unholy fury when she didn't get her way. Her rages were the stuff of legend, eclipsing even their father's bouts of book throwing and furniture tossing. Arthur's temper was reactionary - a pressure release valve that opened when he was pushed beyond his coping threshold. Anya's was part of her original build, baked into the scaffolding of her DNA. It was constitutional wrath, like God of the Old Testament. Worship me or I will flood the world.

For all of Katherine's worry and pearl clutching and Oh My Goodnesses, she still beamed kindness from her core, a self-sustaining fusion reaction that ejected warmth and light out across the vacuum of space. Anya, by contrast, was more like a hurricane. Terrestrial and terrifying, she would swirl and howl and grow as she consumed more hateful fuel, slowly churning over cities and towns, laying waste to them as she passed over. Eventually, she would exhaust herself and disperse back into the air and sea, leaving shell-shocked survivors to climb out of their makeshift shelters to assess the wreckage.

She had punished Ronan before and this was not the first time he'd stared down hectic green skies and a Category 5 Anya on the horizon. But this was her baby, her first cub, and Ronan had made off with him in broad daylight like a stagecoach robber. He wouldn't be surprised if she was calling from one of the pursuing cruisers. Hell, he wouldn't be surprised if she was driving one.

Vengeance is mine. I will repay, says the Lord.

He passed a look to Joel, who merely shrugged his shoulders. Ronan pushed the button to accept the call.

"How was the burial?"

"*You fucking bastard!*"

Her cold wind shrieked through the car, sweeping across them, lifting them up into the twisting cyclone of her soaking rage. The police continued to follow them, the convoy swelling to a dozen vehicles or more. In the distance, they could see the first of the news helicopters arrive on the scene.

Chapter Twenty

An hour later, they crossed into New Haven. Ronan smirked to himself, he couldn't help it. Fowler would never pay up, but the victory was permanent. The mix of Rhode Island and Connecticut State troopers had grown into a fleet of pursuers, with some off-duty vehicles and unmarked SUVs that made Ronan worry about three letter government agencies. At the height of this chase, there were three helicopters from competing news stations following them, but a police helicopter chased them off and was now following some 500 feet above Ronan's Cadillac. A spotlight shone down over them, harsh in the fading daylight. The news helicopters buzzed into and around the police like angry wasps, veering towards them and then away again, fighting a game of inches for the best shot.

Beverly calling.

"This outta be good," Ronan said.

"Who's Beverly?"

"Beverly Winslow is my agent. Did you ever see *The Terminator*?"

Joel nodded.

"Picture a tough-as-nails war machine in orange stilettos and a pant suit, killing her way to fifteen percent."

Ronan punched the button on the dash.

"Hi Bev, what's happening?"

"You're trending is what's happening."

"Oh yeah," Ronan said. "Where's that?"

There was a pause on the other end.

"Everywhere, Ronan. Have you not been watching the news?"

He laughed at her.

"Kind of preoccupied at the moment."

"You should really take a look."

Ronan gestured to his nephew. Joel unlocked his phone and started scrolling, fingers moving faster, his eyes getting wider with each passing second.

"Holy shit, Uncle Ronan, you're all over everything."

Beverly broke in.

"Half of California is rooting for you to make it to NYC. This is all over Twitter. #RunRonanRun. #CannonballRun22. #NYCorbust. #Captiveaudience.

"I like that last one."

"Do you have any idea what this means?"

Ronan laughed at her again, not without a touch of bitterness.

"It means I'm going to prison."

It was her turn to laugh. To Ronan it sounded like a machine gun spitting bullets.

"Oh please! I've got rabid hordes of criminal lawyers made for such an occasion, I assure you. You'll do a year in a country club and then community service and probation."

"You can't be serious."

"Deadly so. Celebrity meltdowns are all the rage right now. You'll be the next Iron Man in three years if you let me work this. But Ronan, be serious with me a moment."

This was ridiculous, all of it, on a level he knew now, he would never understand. He didn't know if he could manage serious, but he tried.

"I'm all ears, Bev."

"You've got everyone's attention right now, Ronan. All eyes are on you. What are you going to do with it?"

Ronan looked at his nephew. Joel was shaking his head, murmuring to himself, lost in scrolling through headlines.

"I'm going to give it all away," he said.

The machine gun fired again.

"Of course you are, Iron Man."

Ronan grinned.

"That does have a nice ring to it."

"Keep your prick up, Ronan, I'm building you an army."

Beverly hung up. He looked out the rearview at the flashing wall of police behind them. At this speed, Bridgeport would be coming up in another ten minutes. He had ignored calls from police commanders and no doubt, hostage negotiators, letting his even speed and nephew's presence do the talking for him. He questioned whether his moral compass had finally gone haywire using Joel as a human shield, but with the press and the reality TV popcorn spectacle that was unfolding, he knew they were wrapped up safe and tight.

But for how much longer?

Fowler had been angry, but Ronan believed him that the police would never let them get into the city. The expense, the manpower, the chaos of shutting down major expressways - there was no way. The highway patrols were already trying to clear the interstate ahead of them and there had to be twenty vehicles tailing them, not to mention the helicopter. When this bill came due, it was going to be light years beyond what he could afford to pay. This insane little jaunt would come to an end sooner or later and Ronan had a sinking feeling it was going to be sooner.

One more call to make before the sand runs through the hourglass.

"You ready for your fifteen minutes?"

Joel looked up from his scrolling, blinking at Ronan as if just noticing him. He gestured around him then to the outside and their diligent pursuers.

"I thought this was the big show."

Ronan shook his head.

"This is just setting the stage, kid. Now we grab the mike and wail."

Joel grinned at him.

"How do we do that exactly?"

"We're going to call in the big guns."

Return to me, Ronan.

He pushed a button. Three thousand miles away, a phone started to ring.

* * *

Margot appeared on the screen between them. Her hair was up in rollers and her makeup looked fresh and expertly applied. She wore a short silk pink robe with a white fur trim. She was smoking a cigarette and flashing her best smile at Ronan.

"Darling. I didn't expect to hear from you for a bit. Everything okay?"

"You busy?"

She blew smoke.

"About to shoot a scene," she said. "But you can have me for a cigarette or two."

"Have you seen the news?"

She presented herself, popping her chest out, hands running alongside her torso.

"You think I wake up like this? I've been in hair and makeup for hours. Are the Reds attacking?"

"Find a TV. You'll see it."

She narrowed her eyes at him, half miffed, half curious.

"You're cutting into my smoke break with reality? I should punish you."

"Will you please just-"

She waved him off.

"Fine. Keep your shirt on, Ike Turner."

She left and Ronan found himself staring at a catering spread and some lawn chairs around a kidney pool. He could hear her in the background, some laughter, other voices and then from somewhere inside, the drone of a television newscast. Her voice broke in from outside the frame. *Holy shit!* He heard a crash, then her laughter *Holy SHIT!* He heard the rapid click of heels on tile and she was back.

"Is this really happening?"

He nodded. She squealed with delight, stamping her feet onto the ground, curlers flying out of her hair in every direction.

"Don't get too excited, I'm going to prison."

She fixed him a devilish grin that spread warmth all the way out to his extremities.

"And you will get conjugal visits that shatter you."

She slipped a tan bare shoulder free from her robe and licked her lips. She reached for the tie of her robe.

"Hey hey, underage kid present."

Joel leaned into the frame, smiling at her sheepishly.

"Hi, I'm Joel. Big fan."

Margot made no attempt to cover up. Instead she leaned back in her seat, letting her robe fall slightly open around the swell of her breasts. She purred at him.

"Well hello," she said. "Aren't you handsome."

Joel blushed furiously, color rising up to his forehead.

"Show Margot your hands, will you?"

He obliged her, holding them out to the console, turning them over in space so she could get a good look.

"You take after your uncle, Joel. Ever thought of coming out to the valley?"

"Seventeen," Ronan said.

She winked at them.

"I'll never tell," she said. "Now what can Margot do for her fans today?"

"What's your strongest social?"

She lit another cigarette and smoked, looking back and forth between them.

"Not the question I was expecting, but okay. Insta probably."

"How many followers?"

She took a drag.

"Twelve million, give or take."

Twelve million!

"What are you thinking, Ronan?"

He put his hand around the back of Joel's neck and squeezed.

"I think we should hand the kid the microphone."

Joel turned.

"Wait. What?"

Then Margot was laughing, clapping her hands together, delighted. Her whole body shook. The last of the curlers shot out of her hair like fireworks. When she regained composure, she watched them for a long moment. Then, with deadly sincerity, she spoke.

"Let's get started gentlemen."

Chapter Twenty-One

J oel fixed his tie in the sun visor mirror while Margot walked them through the technicalities.

"Open the shade for the sunroof."

Ronan pointed up.

"I've got a police helicopter up there."

"Good, we need a key light."

He opened the sunshade and a blinding spotlight shot down at them.

"Too much. Close it halfway."

Ronan drew the shade and the harshness cut out.

"Better. Now do the dome lights over the dash."

He flipped the button on the two map lights and the cabin filled with a soft amber glow.

"Perfect," she said. "Now let's have a look at you."

They leaned into center frame and beamed at her.

"Men never need makeup," she said, frowning. "Know that I despise you both for that. But you look great."

She made an O with her thumb and forefinger. A crowd had gathered behind her, peering down at them from over her shoulder. It was a motley mix of women in robes, sturdy looking men, and tech people. It looked like a whole production crew, staring at the two of them like expectant parents.

"Okay Joel, honey, look at me."

Joel looked into the screen, face serious.

"I know you've got this sheep dog thing going on here. It's cute, but women will want to see your face. Let's see it."

He wiped a mop of hair out of his face and smiled.

"God, you're beautiful."

He blushed again.

"Down girl. What's next?"

Margot tapped her phone with a lacquered fingernail.

"We're going to do an intro for you from here first. I just sent my login info to Joel's phone. I'll text you when we're ready for you. Then you log in as me and we go live on Margot Throbbie Official."

"Okay," Ronan said. "What do I do then?"

She scowled at him.

"You introduce yourself as my boyfriend, describe the scene, and then hand the phone over to the talent. You're acting like you've never done this before."

"Boyfriend."

"Yes darling. Just say your lines and we'll be aces."

He nodded.

"Thank you for doing this. For me. For us."

"You can thank me in person soon. I'm heading to the airport as soon as you go live."

"Are you crazy?"

"Someone's got to post bail for you.

He felt a surge of emotion churning up through his guts, forcing its way up and out through his lips.

"Margot, I-"

She held a hand up to him.

"Stop speaking, Ronan," she said. "Words always ruin it. Don't ruin it. Besides…"

She blew him a kiss.

"I told you this would happen."

The moment was approaching. Joel ran a hand through his hair.

"I don't know what to say, guys."

Margot sat back and assessed him. It was the closest thing to tender Ronan had ever seen in her face and he was struck by how beautiful it was.

"If you're anything at all like your uncle, you're gonna be just fine.

"I-"

"Trust me," she said and then pointed to Ronan. "You. Steer that ship steady. And don't drop the soap until I get there."

She clicked off and there was a moment of silence between them. Joel picked at his teeth.

"You okay?"

Joel nodded.

"Are *you* okay?"

With his dad in the ground and two stints of rehab under his belt, Ronan never expected to feel what he was feeling in that moment. With the tabloids running with his scandalous (*girlfriend?*) lifestyle and the vertigo of standing atop a very high place with no real idea of how he got there and only one way down, he never imagined he'd ever feel right again, but here he was. It wasn't elation or mania or even satisfaction. Not really. It was calmer, more thorough, more total. It wasn't an emotion that rose and fell or peaked and petered out. It was even keel, a deeper, tidal sense that he was playing a role that was written exclusively for him and playing it to perfection.

"I'm okay."

Jesus, I'm really okay.

The car hummed. The police followed. The road lay open. A warm ember of surety burned deep in the very depths of him. He believed, in a simple certain way, perfectly fitting, that Arthur would be proud.

* * *

[Transcript taken from @margothrobbieofficial, October 25th, 2022]

Hi. My name is Joel Schachner. I'm seventeen. I live in New England with my family. I want you all to know that we're safe and I'm okay. My uncle isn't a kidnapper. I've been in a mental hospital for two weeks and my grandfather died. Uncle Ronan broke me out and took me to the funeral. I told him I always wanted to go to New York. I've never been and my folks won't let me go. And there was…some other stuff we needed to work out. I've been in trouble recently, with drugs and depression, I guess. You can't see them, but I have marks under these clothes from trying to hang myself. I don't really think I knew what I was doing at the time. Honestly, I'm not sure what I'm doing now, but I know I don't want to die and that feels like a big step.

I'm not used to talking, like this I mean. I've never had an audience before. I want to say hi to my mom and dad and my sister, Ruth, and my little brother, Benji. Guys, I'm in a car chase! It's like something out of a movie. Also, I met Margot

Throbbie and she is super cool. Like beyond what we all know her for. Way beyond.

I lost my Nonno today. I'm fresh from the service, otherwise I wouldn't be caught dead dressed like this. We used to go to college basketball games together and he taught me how to drive and catch a fastball. When I was little, he would take me to court with him so I could watch him at work. I remember thinking how cool that was. I was a kid, what did I know, right? But he explained everything, down to the smallest details. After, he'd take me to lunch on the water and we'd tell fart jokes until we started getting dirty looks from the other tables. It's funny what you remember about people when they go, I guess.

Anyway, I feel kind of bad. I know you all come on here to check out Margot and now here's this dumb kid instead. I know I'm not what you tuned in for. But I need to say something, so here goes. I feel like a fuckup. I hate myself a lot of the time because I'm so different from everyone around me. I don't care about the shit I'm supposed to care about. I don't feel the same way about school and bullshit like everyone else does. I try to go my own way, but I always feel like someone picks me up and tries to make me fit back into some stupid mold.

I do drugs because that's what you do when you're a kid and you're stuck in your home town and you can't get out into the world. It's not like I'm numbing myself or trying to escape. It's like the exact opposite - I'm trying to feel something, anything other than this shitty feeling of not being what everybody wants me to be.

I love you, Mom. But you push me into all this shit I don't want. Sports. Clubs. Cliques. You cram all this picture perfect stuff down my throat so you can brag to your church group about it, but it isn't me at all. I love you, Dad, but it's like you just don't care. You just check out and go play in your band and you leave me. It's like you're pissed I live with you and you have better things to do. You guys make me feel like Ruth and Benji are perfect and I'm the one who embarrasses you. Do you know what that feels like? Did your parents do that to you? Will I do that to my kids? Man, I hope not.

I thought you'd be better off without me. If I'm being honest and it kinda feels important to be honest right now, I didn't think anyone would really miss me. You could all finally move on and scratch my face out of family photos and pretend like the whole thing never happened. Joel went off to live on a farm with all the other dogs, or some shit.

The more I think about it, that seems pretty stupid though, doesn't it? I talk to people like my uncle and Margot and I realize we're all fuckups, aren't we? They don't apologize for it and I don't think I want to either. I'm different, Mom, Dad. I'm different from you. I used to look at adults and think they all had their shit so together. Like tight. But you don't. You're just big kids with no clue. You're just making it up as you go and now that I see that, I'm kind of rocked that the world continues on. If there are real miracles, mom, that's a big one.

I don't know what happens now. We're going to try to get to New York, but I don't think we'll make it. But we tried. I guess we'll keep trying until we do. Right? Anyway, I think that's it for me. Thanks for listening to me ramble. Thank you to Margot and Uncle Ronan for a chance to talk. This has probably been the greatest day of my life.

[End of transcript]

* * *

They came upon the road block right before Stamford. Police were spread across four lanes of traffic, from the guardrail to the breakdown lane. A line of squad cars and SUVs clustered around a hulking tactical beast that looked like a semi truck from a *Mad Max* movie. What seemed like every SWAT team in Connecticut had their rifles trained on the Cadillac and Ronan felt certain there were snipers, both in the air above them and peppered across the rooftops of the nearby buildings.

End of the line.

He slowed the car, patting himself down for smokes. He freed the pack from his jacket and looked inside. One left. He popped it out and stuck it in the corner of his mouth. He lit it and inhaled deeply. He put an arm on Joel's shoulder and squeezed.

"My friend," he said. "It's been an honor."

Joel looked at him, not smiling, not serious. His eyes shined and he looked ready for whatever came next, a far cry from the stooped and sullen boy who had escaped the hospital that afternoon. He was handsome in his suit and underneath, even now, the marks were healing. The wounds remained and the heavy lifting was yet to come, but these would heal too with time. If nothing else, like everything Ronan did, they were all forced to look at it now. They couldn't sweep it under the rug or pray it away or turn their heads and pretend they didn't see it. It was in their faces now, the trumpets of Anya's furious angels, not to be dismissed.

"I meant what I said, Uncle Ronan."

He put his hand on Ronan's shoulder, squeezing him in return.

"This is the greatest day of my life."

Ronan smoked, trying to get the last of it into his lungs before he brought the car to a stop.

"Remember it, Joel, for the days when things aren't so great. Because there's more of those than these."

Joel was solemn.

"I won't forget."

Ronan tapped the brakes and the car rolled to a halt. The spotlight from the helicopter hovered over them and the world filled with blue and red flashes. A bullhorn screeched to life with a warble of feedback.

"STEP OUT OF THE VEHICLE!"

Joel grabbed his arm.

"Will we be okay?"

Ronan took a final drag, exhaled and closed his eyes.

"Put your hands on the dash and don't move. Just do what they say when they approach the car and you'll be okay."

Police on foot were inching closer to the idling car, rifles out in front of them.

"And you?"

Ronan adjusted his tie and buttoned his suit jacket. He gave Joel the grin that had, like a trademark, come to define just about every single aspect of his life.

"I was built for this," he said and opened the door.

Under the glare of spotlights, splashed by the flashes of strobes, Ronan Besso took the stage and stepped out to meet his audience.

About the Author

GEOFFREY VISGILIO is the award-winning author of *Believe* (2014), *Switch* (2017), and *The Bullshit Artist* (2025). Both intimate and expansive, his work searches out the moments when hidden worlds brush up against our own. His stories wander across borderlands, guided by a fascination with what is hidden in plain sight, moving through landscapes of rupture and renewal, love and estrangement, and forces beyond our understanding. A Rhode Island native, Geoffrey lives in Providence, where he communes with spirits, both ethereal and distilled.

If you enjoyed this story and want to see more like it, please leave a review for Geoffrey on your favorite platform.